WICKED LOVE

USA TODAY BESTSELLING AUTHOR

EMMANUELLE SNOW

Smart Lily
Publishing

Wicked Love
Emmanuelle Snow

First edition - December 2023 (V_1) (update 2025)

ISBN eBook: 978-1-998077-19-9

ISBN paperback: 978-1-998077-20-5

Editors: Shalini G.

Cover: SMART Lily Publishing inc.

Published by SMART Lily Publishing inc.

⫷◈⫸⭒⫷◈⫸

Emmanuelle Snow
emmanuellesnow.com

CARTER HILLS BAND UNIVERSE
(SUGGESTED READING ORDER)

Carter Hills Band series
False Promises

HEART SONG DUET
Blindsided
Forevermore

Whiskey Melody series
Sweet Agony

SECOND TEAR DUET
Cruel Destiny
Beautiful Salvation

BREATHLESS DUET
Wild Encounter
Brittle Scars

Upon A Star series
Last Hope

Midnight Sparks

Love Song For Two series
<u>Lonesome Heart Duet</u>
Fallen Legend
Rising Star

<u>Two of Us Duet</u>
Snowbound

Wicked Love

All titles available at
emmanuellesnow.com

For the best experience, read in the order as shown above

TRIGGER WARNINGS

Disclaimer

My books are realistic and emotional love stories.

I'm an advocate for mental health, and some topics could be sensitive for certain readers since they are portrayed as close to real life as possible.

I've listed the potential trigger warnings for each title on my website.

Be advised that those trigger warnings could potentially be spoiler alerts for the storylines.

Those sensitive topics have been written with the utmost care and respect. Please reach out if you have questions or comments.

All books contain sexuality, mature content, and language not intended for people under 18 years of age.
For other readers' sake, please avoid spoilers in your reviews.

Thank you and have a wonderful day!

Emmanuelle

emmanuellesnow.com

You're never too old to believe in fairytales and magic.

I prefer love to war, don't you?

BECOME A VIP

TO NEVER MISS A THING

Snow's VIP

Join **Emmanuelle Snow's VIP newsletter** for all the cool stuff, promos, new releases, giveaways, and gifts.

emmanuellesnow.com

Snow's Soulmates

Join Emmanuelle Snow's Facebook VIP group, **Snow's Soulmates**, to chat with her and other readers, get updates, and more bonus content.

facebook.com/groups/snowvip

NOT A SNOWSTORM
THE SONG

It's cold, and the snow has been
    falling all night, baby
Covering the sidewalks in white
    shiny powder
No, I don't wanna go to work today
We should stay in and snuggle
    all day
It's better to push everything else to
    later
The best days are when we're alone,
    just you and me

[CHORUS]

Wake up, baby, it's snowing outside
Let's catch snowflakes with our
    tongues
And dance like there is no tomorrow
Being snowed in with you feels like
We're lost in our own little bubble

Where nothing else but us exists
Let's play outside, then I'll warm
    you up
(Oh, yes, I'll warm you up by the
    fireplace)

It's not a snowstorm, but I wish it
    could be, baby
The town would close, and we'd stay
    here forever
I don't wanna do anything else
    today
Let's drink hot chocolate and watch
    movies all day
The weather doesn't bother me as
    long as we're together
There's no rush, no place else I'd
    rather be

[CHORUS]
Loving you is the easiest thing I've
    ever done in my life
There's nothing like the feel of you
    nestled in my arms at night
I wish we could be snowed in
    every day
And stay in our little world for the
    rest of time
Baby, I never thought I would love
    snow more than I do today
And it made me realize I never
    wanna go away (no, I never
    wanna go away)

Let's pretend it's snowing for
    eternity
So we don't have to ever leave this
    place (no, never leave this place)

[CHORUS]
The snow has stopped, we gotta
    wake up, baby
There's not a single trace outside of
    the white cover
I wish we could still be snowed in
    today
So I wouldn't have to get on with
    my life all day
It still feels like it was all a dream,
    that I made up the weather
Can we go back to yesterday and
    have a do-over maybe?

Let's get back to bed and pretend
    we're snowed in again
For the rest of time, we'll stay here
    and love each other
Baby, don't open your eyes
Let's get back to bed and pretend
    we're snowed in again
If only for one more day (One more
    day together)

Music and lyrics by Anderson Ford

Chapter 1

With my elbows propped up on the cold surface of the worn walnut countertop, I people-watched the patrons surrounding me. Some were in this dive bar to get shit-faced. Others were here for a late-night drink with friends. I was part of the first group. My dad had requested I come home this weekend, and I felt no joy whatsoever meeting with him. Sure, I adored my dad. He was the coolest guy I knew, but I wasn't pleased with the direction his new life was taking, and even though I had thrown every argument at him, he still remained blind to the truth. A part of me feared that he would announce the thing I dreaded the most this weekend. A little liquid courage and a night in a hotel would prevent me from facing the harsh reality tonight. Tomorrow could wait. For now.

The air smelled of cigarettes and cheap beer, as if the

smoke over the years had welded with the paint and furniture and never dissipated.

Rock music from the seventies played in the background, just loud enough to fill the space but not so loud as to be distracting. More like a gentle hum in the background.

I hadn't visited Dick's Hole often in my life. The name of the bar alone was the first telltale sign of how crappy it was. Everything around me looked dirty and old as fuck. As if it came from another era. If depression could be a place, no doubt it'd be Dick's Hole on Fourth Avenue in a small Pennsylvania town, a thirty-mile drive from my hometown of Silverville.

The place was filled with mismatched wooden chairs that looked as though they were on the brink of collapsing from exhaustion, weathered wooden tables, their surfaces so uneven that leaving a drink unattended seemed like a gamble, a dusty jukebox that had probably not seen a quarter in ages, and ripped black vinyl stools lining the bar. The majority of the crowd could've been my grandparents, save for a few missing teeth and the stories etched on their faces. I used to spend time at Dick's Hole during my senior year of high school because they never checked IDs, and my friends and I could get drunk for cheap.

A girl with long bleached blonde hair sat in a corner, three empty beer bottles aligned on the table before her. She looked as out of place here as I felt.

She peeled the label of the bottle in her hand, seemingly lost in her thoughts, her eyes haunted.

I took in the black lines around her eyes and the dark shadows coloring her eyelids. She was wearing a cut-off vintage band T-shirt that exposed her midriff, paired with a mini black faux-leather skirt and knee-high boots. She looked nothing like the girls I hooked up with, but there was just something about her that enticed me. An air of sadness clinging to her features—a distinctive vulnerability —that made me want to know more. To uncover her truths and her secrets.

For some reason, I couldn't seem to look away from her. In my head, I imagined what her story could be. Had she been dumped? Or had she just learned her dog ran away? Or maybe she lived with evil stepsisters and needed a night of reprieve?

She turned my way, and I noticed how pretty she looked. High cheekbones, straight nose, pillowy lips. Too bad she felt like she had to hide under her black armor as if it protected her from the world.

I savored the whiskey as it slid over my tongue while scrolling through my phone, lost in thought, until a low battery notification flashed on the screen. Fucking great.

I got up, careful to not touch anything, and weaved around the tables toward the restroom. A man and a woman in their late fifties were making out—full tongue and groping hands—by the restroom door. In the point two seconds I looked their way, I swore I saw both their tonsils as they were about to eat each other out without an ounce of discretion.

Glad they could get some.

I'd been a monk lately. Since I'd started my new job in New York, I had the opportunity to fuck as much as I liked, yet I kept pushing away all the women showing an interest in me.

Perhaps I needed that. A reprieve. After fucking my way through college, maybe my dick needed a more than deserved vacation.

Behind me, people started cheering, and I turned around, wondering what the commotion was about.

Hurrying back to my stool, I watched the girl, who had

been nursing a drink alone, standing on the bar and guzzling vodka straight from the bottle. I noticed a butterfly tattoo peeking out from under the waistband of her skirt.

"Chug. Chug. Chug," everyone chanted as she wiped her mouth with the back of her hand. She threw both arms in the air and did a victory dance. Tipsy, she wobbled on her feet, while most patrons were either too oblivious or too drunk to notice.

I hurried over and caught her, honeymoon style, before she hit the floor.

"*Myyy* hero," she singsonged, her voice low and intoxicated.

"I'm nobody's hero."

She looped her arms around my neck. "I…I beg to differ. *Youuu're* mine."

"You're welcome."

"I-I think I am…huh…dead." She stared into my eyes and nodded as if to convince herself.

"You look pretty alive to me. Sloshed. But alive."

"*Youuu* look like an angel. A troublesome angel, but—" She studied my face, squinting. "A…a badass angel. One who can't behave but *lovvves* every minute of it." A hiccup. She placed a hand over her mouth, her cheeks turning an adorable shade of pink. "*Sorrry*. What was I saying…? Oh *yesss*, that *youuu* are beautiful."

I snorted. "Beautiful? Maybe you're more drunk than I thought."

"Men are allowed to be…to be beautiful too, *youuu* know? We're not in nineteen sixty anymore. Just say *thaaank* you."

"Thanks."

"*Youuu're* sure I'm alive? I-I feel cold."

I looked at her, unsure how she had managed to fascinate me in just a minute. I couldn't tear my eyes away from her figure. With her in my arms, I had an undeniable view of her cleavage, the band T-shirt she wore failing to conceal the swell of her breasts and the black lace of her bra.

My body tensed in the best of ways, and I grinned. "To me, you feel hot."

"Oh, *youuu* are a smooth talker," she gushed, batting her eyelashes, her gaze following my line of vision as I admired her voluptuous curves. "Are *youuu…* Are you ogling *meee*?"

I shrugged. "Maybe."

"*Youuu* have no shame. That's refreshing. I-I think I'm in *lovvve*," she declared, slurring her words.

"Good for you. I prefer love to war, don't you?" I chuckled, not drunk enough to engage in her line of conversation. "Well, when tomorrow comes, you may change your mind."

She toyed with the locks of my hair, twisting them between her fingers, sending an electric jolt all the way down to my toes.

Before I could reel it in, a growl escaped my lips, every inch of me relishing the attention a little too much.

Her gaze traveled the length of my arms, and it felt like a burning caress. She eyed my white T-shirt as if staring at it long enough would dissolve the fabric.

"Love what you see?" I grinned, unable to resist engaging with her.

She pinched her lips together, her cheeks turning a shade darker. "Those pecs *youuu* have are hard. *Veryyy* hard. I *lovvve* hard body parts. It means… It means *youuu* work them out well."

I coughed in surprise. "You love *hard body parts*?"

She bobbed her head. "Always. I-I'm telling *youuu*. Don't you agree?"

I gazed at the spot where her tits pressed against my chest. "Well, I love soft flesh better. And anything that's moist."

"*Ohhh.*"

I winked. "You started it."

"It…it takes two to play." She raised two fingers and squinted at them as if to make sure she had the right count. "Doesn't it?" She grinned at me.

"Who said I wanted to play?"

"No need, I-I can tell. Wanna know a *secrrret?*" she asked, lowering her voice and bringing her mouth closer to my ear as I leaned in. Her booze-filled breath tickled my cheek. "I…I think we're getting along *juuust* fine. Do *youuu* think I-I'm pretty?"

I swallowed. "Yeah, you are."

The air between us was charged with awareness.

"Then *youuu* and I, we…huh…we should kiss," the girl, still in my arms, announced, keeping her voice low. "I think it's a *greaaat* idea."

"You do?" Why were her words sending surges of heat through me? If this girl thought I was a troublemaker, then she hadn't looked at herself in the mirror in a long fucking-ass time. From the full juicy lips to the rack she sported and the way she batted her eyelashes like it was her full-time job, she had sex written all over her features. Wild nights and filthy dreams. There was no way I could ever stay indifferent to her. No matter how hard I tried.

"*Yesss.*" She licked her lips, her eyes never faltering. "Don't *youuu?*"

I could imagine ten different things those lips could do right now, and none of them were G-rated.

I did my best to stay still and not show how desperate I

was for a taste of her. "I think you're too drunk and need to switch to water."

"Well, *youuu*—"

"Joe."

"Well, Joe. I-I need a break from *myyy* life tonight. I...I got exiled from the only life I'd ever known against my will, and a...a booze-induced night is *goood* for me. It makes me happy...and relaxed. I wanna forget *everythhhing* for a few hours."

My senses were on high alert. "Have you been like kidnapped or something?" Geez, in what fucked-up situation had I landed in? Could she really be in danger, or was she joking? My brain was a mushy mess, and thinking clearly was harder than it should have been.

"*Meee*? Nope." She glided her jaw back and forth. "If *youuu* think about it, in-in some way...kidnapping sounds... huh...about right, though."

"Stop messing with me. Is someone hurting you? Or making you do stuff you're not comfortable with? Be honest."

Something flashed in her gaze, but it vanished as quickly as it appeared. "*I'mmm* fine. Don't worry about *meee*. It...it was just an expression. I am... I am in no physical danger."

Why did I sense a but? Perhaps I was too wasted right now to really analyze her facial features, and I read her wrong. "You would tell me if you were in trouble?"

"Joe, *youu* are the sweetest guy I've ever met." She kissed my cheek, her lips lingering on my flesh longer than needed. My body awoke at the contact. The girl never answered the question, and I decided to let it go. For now.

"I'm not known for being sweet."

"*Ohhh*. And what are *youuu* known for?"

"It's a secret. And one for you to find out."

"*Youuu're* funny. My mother has decided to *packkk* her stuff and move across the country in the name of true *lovvve*…or…huh, her definition of it. I came here with her. End. Of. Story." She paused for a long moment, and something close to defeat shone in her eyes. "I-I didn't really have a say in the matter."

"Your mother? How old are you?"

"Old enough to drink in a place called *Dickkk's* Hole." She squinted. "Why do *youuu* think they named it *that*? I'm…I'm not sure it's not creepy."

I shrugged. "Who knows? It's been an establishment in this town forever. Nobody knows the real story behind its name."

"*O-kay*." She paused, seemingly to think. "You-you live here?"

"Used to. I live in New York now."

"Are *youuu* like famous or something?"

"I wish, but no. I'm a musician. On Broadway. I play the piano in musicals."

Her eyes grew big like saucers. "Whoa. *Youuu* do?"

"Yep."

Lowering her down, I gripped her arm, waiting for her to steady herself on her feet.

"You good?" I asked.

"*Suuure*." She scrunched up her nose, studying me. "I-I think you're really *cuuute*. For a pianist."

"What does that mean?"

She rolled her eyes as if I were exasperating her. "I… I… What was I saying? Oh *yesss*. I told *youuu* already you're beautiful. Would you prefer I tell *youuu* you're hot?"

"Yeah. Definitely."

She took one of my hands in hers, examining my digits. "*Youuu* have long pianist's fingers. I…I bet you can do a *lottt* of things with those."

Was she serious right now? Never before had a girl compared my piano skills to sex. There was just something about this one that aroused every inch of my body. Her sultry voice, her confidence, her sex-appeal, her entire being. I couldn't explain it or pinpoint where it came from, but somehow, she was seeping under my skin without my realizing it.

"Too bad you'll never know," I teased.

We fixated our gazes on each other, neither of us blinking. The tension swirling between us sparkled with heat. Why was I unable to let her walk away?

"You sure you're old enough to drink?" My voice sounded rough. I coughed, trying to get rid of the lust thickening my vocal cords.

She cupped her mouth and leaned closer, her chest brushing against mine. In her two-inch high heels, she was only a couple of inches shorter than I. Her scent, fresh and herbal, teased my nose. "Good genes. One day, I'll be grateful that I…that I look younger than *myyy* age. For the record, I-I'm not really twenty-one, but *I'mmm* an adult, so who cares, right?"

"I won't snitch on you."

She did some kind of military salute, two fingers pressed against her forehead. "Thank *youuu*, sir."

"I went from cute pianist to sir?"

She giggled, the clear sound regaling my ears, and took my hand between hers. Her touch injected me with a sense of calm I'd never experienced before.

"Why are *youuu* spending the night in a *shittty* bar, Joe? You looked lonely earlier. I-I'm sure there are *muchhh* more enjoyable places for *youuu* to be, no?"

Why did it surprise me that she noticed me too? Since I'd arrived, I had barely been able to detach my gaze from her.

"My dad. He's the best man I know, but now he lives in a plastic world, and it saddens me. Not that he is a plastic guy, but soon he'll turn into one. Anyway, he asked me to come home this weekend. I'm here only for him, but I needed to take the edge off first…and…huh…avoid getting home too soon."

"I get it. *Myyy* mom is a nutcase. I…I wish we were not related most of the time."

We sat at the bar, and I ordered two glasses of water.

"*Youuu* don't need to keep playing lifesaver," the girl said. "I'm…I'm smart enough to stop drinking when I *reachhh* my limit."

"Which is?"

"*Jussst* before I puke. I-I hate puking; it's *grosss*. And it smells."

I couldn't keep inside the laugh that bubbled out. This girl was a walking contradiction. Sexy and confident enough to get all the guys here to notice her, yet innocent enough to sound like she needed saving. Never before had a girl amused me the way she did. "Duly noted."

She raised a hand to wave the bartender over. "Two *shotsss* of tequila."

I frowned. "Tequila? You sure it's a good idea?"

Her smile reached both ears. "I-I'm having fun. *Youuu* chased away the dark clouds of *myyy* night. I wanna make the most of it." She blinked, and when she stared back at me, lust flashed in her eyes. Something I bet my own eyes reflected. "Don't you *wannna* just have fun and let loose?"

She slid the straw between her candy-red painted lips, and I wondered how they would feel wrapped around me. Could this girl, with a wicked sense of humor and brutal honesty, cure me of my dry spell? My gaze traced the curve of her breasts once again, unable to resist the creamy flesh bulging right in front of me. Yup, I was cured. And I hoped it was a permanent fix.

The bartender put the shot glasses in front of us.

"To avoiding parents *annnd* living our best life," the girl cheered.

We both downed the liquor in one go and tapped our glasses against the bar.

The sad girl with haunted eyes I spotted earlier had been pushed aside. Before me sat a girl with rosy cheeks and bright eyes in a drunken haze.

"*Thankkks* for getting me out of whatever funk I-I was in earlier," she told me, all traces of humor gone from her features. "And thank *youuu* for the company. I had a shitty day and an even shittier week. It-it's fun to have someone to talk to. I feel…I feel mostly invisible, defective, or alone in this new house I live in. Other than to blame *meee*, my mother doesn't care about what I do or where I go. As long as I look the *parrrt*."

I rested my hand over hers and gave it a squeeze. Heat pulsed between our connected skin. "You never told me your name?" I asked, trying to bring back the easy conversation we shared seconds ago.

"*Ooops*." She held out her hand. "Isla. Isla De la Durantaye. Nice to officially meet *youuu*, Joe."

I met her palm and shook her proffered hand, more heat creeping up my arm. "De la Durantaye. It sounds French. Are you from Europe?"

"*Caaanada*. My grandparents. *Lonnng* story. What about *youuu*?"

"My mom was from Maryland and my dad, from here. Nothing super exciting." I moved to my feet. "Give me a sec? I gotta take a leak."

She flicked her wrist. "Yeah. Go ahead. I-I'll get more

booze." She flashed me a smile, and I couldn't find it in me to refuse.

Perhaps a hangover would make whatever my dad wanted to talk about tomorrow easier.

She pivoted on the stool, and all her attention shifted to the bartender as she animatedly placed the order using both hands.

I gave a wry smile and walked toward the restroom, my heart thudding a little harder with excitement.

With one last look in the mirror mounted above the restroom sink, I took in the exhaustion shadowing my eyes and tightening my features. Since I'd graduated from college, I had been working like crazy. And now I could see the signs. With rehearsals for the new show that would go live next spring and three performances a day, I rarely banked more than five hours of sleep at night these days. But I loved what I was doing, so I couldn't complain. I just needed a few days to relax and a good fuck, and I'd be brand new. The recessed light in the ceiling strobe and the plumbing groaned with a noise straight out of a horror movie. Dick's Hole hadn't gotten better over the years; that was for sure.

A knock on the door snapped me out of my thoughts.

After drying my hands, I unlocked the door, only to be met by a pair of brown eyes twinkling in the dim light.

"You?"

Isla strode forward and pushed my chest back with her tiny hands, forcing me to retreat into the barely sanitary bathroom, stumbling on my own feet.

My back collided with the wall, and she spun on herself, locking the door behind her.

When she turned around, we fixated on each other, neither of us blinking. Her irises shone with lust. And desperation. A need to forget. For a minute…a night…or maybe longer.

I sucked in a breath, waiting for her to say something, but she remained silent.

"Care to explain?" I asked with a cocked brow after a moment, not drunk enough to do whatever she asked of me in *here*.

She pursed her lips, that begged to be kissed, and stalked closer.

My dick stirred in my pants.

"I…I've had time to think about it. *Annnd* it is final. I want *youuu* to *fuckkk* me," she said matter-of-factly as if she had just informed me about the weather.

I lifted my hands in surprise. "I was gone for what? Two minutes? Weren't you supposed to order drinks during that time? "

"I-I was… But…huh…I changed *myyy* mind right before I did. Now I *wannnt* to get drunk on *youuu* instead of booze."

"Isn't that a bit presumptuous? Cornering me in the men's restroom and asking me to bang you?"

She took a step back, hurt flashing in her eyes, and crossed her arms over her chest, pushing her tits almost out of her top. "*Youuu* look like a decent enough guy who's… huh…not all about his own pleasure *annnd* can get the girl there too. *Youuu* cared about me earlier. Remember when I…when I said you were sweet? *Annnd* hot. Well, sweet guys are not egoistical *jerrrks*. And hot guys know how to bring a *girrrl* to orgasm. See? Perfect combination. We-we already proved there is chemistry between us. *Whaaat* more do you want? Are *youuu* in?"

She studied my face, searching for the reaction I refused to give her, as I schooled my features—or I hoped I did. Sometimes, my drunken brain imagined things that hadn't really happened.

"You want me to fuck you?" I perused the space around me, disgusted by the lack of cleanliness surrounding us. "In here?" I had to make sure I heard her right and it wasn't some kind of hallucination.

"Yeah. Where else? *Youuu* know of a secret room in the bar I…I know nothing about? Don't act all prissy and stuff. We-we don't have to touch anything. *Youuu* can hold me in *youuur* arms. See? Anyway, I won't let you push inside *meee* in the hallway like the lady just outside this door, so this is like…huh…this is the best option."

"Ugh. I can't believe they're still at it."

"Yeah. *Annnd* when I came over, he had her bent against the old payphone. Not a thing I…I want my brain to remember in the morning." She took a step closer. "But *youuu*, I could do with remembering." She combed a lock of my hair back with her hand, and once again, I shivered at the contact.

"Seriously, how old are you?" I asked, not wanting to add "creep" to my long list of fuck-ups, as I doubted she was old enough to vote.

She rolled her eyes. "Told *youuu*, good genes. Better to look young than old. If you must know, I-I'll turn nineteen in December." Moving into my space, she trailed kisses up my neck, stopping by my earlobe. My body stiffened with need under her delicate touch. "What do *youuu* say, Joe? Wanna make *meee* come tonight?"

Desire washed through me at the way my name rolled off her tongue. Her voice sounded like dirty promises. My dick fucking loved it.

If I agreed, it wouldn't be the first time I hooked up with a stranger I had no intention of ever seeing again.

Still, there was something about this girl that told me to be gentle.

"College?" I asked to make sure I wasn't doing anything illegal if I got her naked.

She exhaled loudly. "*Takkking* some time off. To reassess what I wanna do with *myyy* life."

"O-okay."

"So, Joe, are *youuu* gonna take me? How long does a *girrrl* have to beg you for *youuu* to fuck her to oblivion?"

She licked a line from my ear to my jaw, and when her mouth pushed against mine, I knew there would be no turning back. This girl had awoken something in me. Fireworks. And an ache I thought I'd never ever feel again.

She screamed trouble, yet it lit me up from the inside out.

I closed my hands around her rounded hips and pulled her toward me, letting her feel how hard I was just from our conversation.

I ground my hips against hers, relishing the tingles the friction provided.

Soft whimpers left Isla's mouth, and they were my undoing.

My lips captured hers. All the hair on my nape stood on end. Isla kissed me back, looping her arms around my neck. My toes curled when our tongues tangoed together— and it sealed the deal. It was one of those searing kisses that branded your soul and changed the rhythm of your heart. The ones you heard about but sounded like a myth since not a lot of people experienced them in their lifetime. I had no idea how to interpret it right now, but I knew for a fact I wouldn't return to my hotel alone.

I lifted my head, and I felt an acute sense of withdrawal as soon as our lips broke apart. "Fuck," I muttered under my breath.

Isla watched me with big eyes, her lipstick smudged around her mouth, and she looked like I'd just branded her as mine. It made no sense even though I liked the idea.

Cupping her cheek with one hand, I traced her bottom lip with my thumb, relishing the shivers that worked through her. "If we're doing this, we're doing it right. I'm not always a gentleman, but I'm not a jerk either. I have a hotel room which is a two-minute walk from here. No way am I fucking you in this place. You deserve better."

I scanned the space around me once more, and no amount of alcohol could make me forget the filthiness of this place.

Dick's Hole.

Yeah, the bar wore its name perfectly.

She followed my line of vision. "Yeah, well… This place is terrible. I think a hotel is a much better idea."

I intertwined our fingers. "Then follow me."

Kicking the door shut, I pushed Isla against it, my lips hungry for hers. We kissed like we were at war. Mortal enemies trying to get the upper hand. My body pulsated. Two hands were not enough to touch her everywhere I yearned to. I had no idea what it was about this girl, but it'd been a long time since I felt alive kissing a stranger. In college, I usually went for the wealthy heiresses or the over-confident bimbos, who cared about nobody but themselves. Isla, though, looked like no one I'd ever been attracted to before. She had a *Stay away, I could be lethal* warning plastered all around her. At the same time, she was like a cute kitten who had claws but didn't know how to use them. At least, not yet. I had no idea if she could ruin me, but for once, I wanted to play with fire. To know how combusting in flames felt like.

Lifting an arm, I fisted her hair, tilting her head back as I devoured her greedy mouth. She tasted like tequila and mint.

I wrapped my other arm around her waist, keeping her as close to me as possible.

Taking control of the situation, Isla unwound the arm holding her and guided it to her thighs. She shoved her skirt up, and with a firm grip on my hand, showed me the way to her wet heat.

She cried as I shunted her panties and pushed a digit inside her tight channel.

Her head jerked back.

Time stopped.

"Fuck, you're soaked."

This girl was my kryptonite. And every whimper exiting her red lips sent a surge of desire through me.

Enveloping my hand with hers, Isla guided my digit in and out of her at a quick pace, chasing her own pleasure. That was so hot. And yet I didn't want to be done too early, the night still young.

"More," she said against my lips. Her low, pleasured voice sent discharges of electricity through me.

Breaking away from the kiss, she bit my earlobe.

"Ouch. Jesus, girl." The sting of pain got me harder. Gone was her good-girl persona, and upfront was her temptress side.

She rolled her hips, searching for friction by locking a foot around my ankle, grinding against me. "Don't…don't you dare go slow," she urged between cries.

Removing my other hand from her hair, I clamped it around her ass, keeping her as close to me as possible and enjoying the flesh filling my palm, as I fingered her with abandon.

I accelerated the pace, my hand a drenched mess.

Her fingernails dug into my shoulders. No doubt they would leave marks. The sadistic part of me relished the fact she was branding me. I loved the idea I was hers for the night.

Isla ate my face, licking and biting. She sampled every inch of my flesh with her greedy tongue, moaning as she did. If kissing her felt this amazing, I had no doubt sex with her would be out of this world.

I couldn't wait to discover if she would consume my entire body with that much passion. Fuck.

An animalistic growl broke free from my throat.

She whimpered in pleasure, and my dick grew harder in my jeans. This had to be the rawest form of desire I'd ever experienced. A carnal hunger I wasn't strong enough to resist.

There was no slowing down or taking things easy.

I had no memory of kissing a girl as if my life depended on it before.

Her lips returned to mine, and my tongue pushed inside her mouth, taking and giving with the same hunger.

Insatiable, I glided a second finger inside her and with my thumb, drew circles over her clit. Isla stiffened against me, and I used this moment to feed on her neck. I sucked the skin there, longing to mark her. I curved my fingers still buried deep inside her and hit her where I knew she wouldn't be able to resist for long. I licked a trail from her collarbone to her jawline. A loud cry parted her lips, and she detonated in my arms, looking beautiful with her head tilted back, hooded eyelids over glazed brown irises.

Unable to stay put any longer and wanting to be buried balls-deep inside her, I fetched a condom from my wallet and rolled it over my strained erection. When I stared at Isla, she was busy ditching all her clothes as if they burned her skin, leaving her in nothing but a set of black bra and panties.

My jaw hung open. She was a sight for sore eyes.

If I thought she looked sexy fully dressed, the half-naked version of her was enough to bring me to my knees.

Lust dripped from her gaze.

Her pupils were fully dilated now, her eyes appearing black.

Her lips were swollen, and gone was her lipstick.

Her tits were a handful, and her hips screamed for me to hold on to them, demanding I punish her for hours to come.

My dick thickened inside my fist, leaking at the tip, and I kicked off my pants and removed my shirt in record time.

"You're a wet dream," I said, stalking her like a hunter after his prey, my gaze focused on her and my mouth watering. "You're gorgeous. And mine for the night."

Starving for her, we tumbled on the mattress in a jumble of limbs, our hands busy traveling all over each other's bodies.

I flipped us over until I could hover over her, staring into her eyes.

Isla propped herself up on her elbows, her mouth desperate for mine. It wasn't passion we shared, but a desperate need. Something to give us a break from the shit-show of our lives for a little time.

In one slow stroke, I lodged myself between her thighs, relishing the moist heat coating my cock.

I crashed my lips down on hers, bruising them, making her whimper.

Meeting me thrust for thrust, I lost myself inside her, forgetting about the rest of the world.

"Harder," she purred, and I delivered, ramming into her with everything I had. Until we both climbed over the edge and fell on the other side, spent and satisfied.

With a sheet covering her naked body, she moved to her feet once we both came down the rush. "Mind if I shower before I go? It's a thirty-minute drive to get home, and I wanna feel fresh when I see my mother. She tends to be judgmental. If she thinks I've been out, she'll go batshit crazy. I would prefer to avoid poking the bear."

I shook my head. "Go ahead. I get it. I got into an argument with my dad earlier. That's what put me in a sour mood. He's being an idiot, and he refuses to see it. Sometimes, I feel like I'm the only adult in this relationship."

She stood by the bed, nodding. "What does your mom say?"

I clamped my nape. "She died. A few years back. My dad is now dipping his dick where he shouldn't. I'm tired of saving him from himself."

"That sucks. My parents are divorced. I don't remember my dad." She rocked on her heels. "My mother is a lot… I can't wait to be out of there and spread my own wings. I'm tired of her belittling everything I do. My body, my clothes, my choices, my life." She flicked her wrist. "Anyway, I'll shower and get out of your way."

Without another word, she entered the bathroom and clicked the door shut after her.

I was right earlier. This girl hid between dark clothes and makeup. It was a shield, an armor. She was protecting herself until she was ready to be her own person.

Jumping to my feet, I knocked on the bathroom door. "Hey Isla, wanna spend the night?"

I blinked. What was I doing? I was so out of my element here. I never invited girls over if I didn't have to.

And yet something about her, call it vulnerability, made me want to hold on to her for a little longer. I was certain she needed the affection just as much as I did.

Dressed in one of my T-shirts minutes later, she slipped under the covers and nestled against my side. I wrapped my arm around her, and before I could think about what I was doing, I kissed the side of her head.

I had no idea what it was about Isla that called to every part of me, but I recognized a loneliness in her that matched mine. As we lay together, a new sense of calm invaded me. I felt better than I had in a long time. Thinking about it, I couldn't pinpoint the last time I'd been at peace.

Soon my body grew heavy, and I drifted to sleep, holding the girl dozing in my arms a little tighter, not ready to let go of her.

When I woke up the next morning, ready to face my father, Isla's perfume still lingered on the sheets, but she was gone. And for a short moment, after what she told me about her mother, I was worried about the girl I knew nothing about.

Chapter 2
Grace

"Grace, no. You can't dress like this. Go and change, or we'll be late again. Please put on something that doesn't make you look like you gained fifteen pounds in the last week." My mother brought her hand to her forehead. Yeah, I was exhausting her, and yet I had done nothing but put on the little blue dress I had bought last summer. Even so, it was still wrong. "And while you're at it, wash your hair. It looks like you haven't done so in two days. Two days, Grace. This is inappropriate. Even for you. Gosh, you're going to bring me to an early death."

Early death.

How many times had I heard her saying the same exact thing since I was old enough to understand her words? Mom had been a runway sensation back when she was eighteen. She hadn't eaten carbs in over twenty years and still watched each calorie entering her body every day.

To her great despair, I was born with thick hips, no gap between my thighs, and a stature more like a bodybuilder than the only daughter of a pageant queen.

Last month, in a moment of rebellion, I had bleached my brown hair and switched the proper demoiselle makeup for thick kohl lines and dark eyeshadows.

Let's just say it hadn't been well-received.

My mother always expected me to be picture-perfect for any occasion.

Now, my dark roots showed, and I didn't know whether I should dye my hair back to its original brown hue or fix the roots. I knew it grated on her last nerve, but I didn't care. Each time she booked me a hair appointment, I found a way out of it.

"What time are we leaving?" I asked, putting as much annoyance into my tone as I could muster, and crossed my arms over my chest.

"Six twelve," Mom said.

"Six twelve? Geez, can you be less precise, please?" I rolled my eyes, wishing she'd noticed. And yet she was already too busy inspecting her manicure to give me any more attention. "It's like three fifteen now. I think I have enough time to get ready later."

Mom sighed. "You should plan ahead. At least two hours for dressing, hair, and makeup. Grace, you know the drill."

"*You can never look too perfect,*" I repeated the words she had told me my entire life.

"Exactly. What about time to shower, wash your hair, do your routine, and any setbacks? You'd better start now. It's going to take you over three hours. Don't neglect your appearance. First impressions are the most important."

"And you want me to impress whom? The hostess? The servers? Or maybe your boyfriend?"

She glared at me.

"We're having a family dinner in a restaurant. I'm not gonna be crowned Queen of England."

"Tonight, you're meeting your brother."

I snorted. "My brother?"

"Yes, Philip's son. I would very much like for him to think you're a well-behaved young lady rather than some wannabe rock star in your…your rebel make-up and punk-band shirts." She scrunched up her nose as if the mere idea of my not dressing as a runway model repulsed her.

"And you want me to impress my *brother* why? And, by the way, we're not related, so brother sounds kind of creepy. He's Phil's son, nothing more to me."

"Philip, Grace. Not *Phil.*" She said *Phil* as if she was about to die from food poisoning.

"Fine. Anyway, his *son* is not my *brother*. And we're not a happily-ever-after family either. I'm heading off to college next year. I'm just biding my time here for now."

Mom and I moved in with Philip two months ago. I had drunk my sorrows for a few days after he flew us from Texas to Pennsylvania. I didn't like it here. Sure, the house was nice enough. Three-story, red-bricked exterior, and white columns with a large, fenced backyard. Four garage doors. And a semi-circled driveway big enough to park ten cars. The inside was all white walls and marble floors. I had my own bedroom with an en-suite bathroom and a Juliet balcony at the back of the house. My *brother* didn't live here but had a room down the hall, similar to mine, for when he visited, which by now had been never. I couldn't blame him. He met my mother once and probably got scarred for life. Our parents' bedroom occupied the entire third floor. It included a media room, a small gym—there was a bigger one on the main floor by the garage—a jacuzzi, a terrace, and a beauty station worthy of a movie set. My mother's dreams.

As much as my mother was a snob, Philip was the most normal man she had ever dated. He didn't care about money or fancy cars. He bought them because he could, not to flash his wealth. It was my mom who had insisted they join the country club. It was also she who begged him to get a maid—and a chef. Why Philip indulged her, I couldn't tell. Their relationship was a mystery to me, yet they seemed perfectly happy.

I entered the kitchen, looking for a snack. One I was aware would be confiscated if Mom caught me. But a girl was allowed to try. Risks made things more interesting. And after my night of binge drinking, I required some sugar to ease the tumble in my stomach.

After waking up with a hangover and a smile—something that rarely occurred nowadays—I came back here with a to-go coffee cup I picked up on the way, pretending I had woken up early because I had a caffeine craving. My mother was so focused on herself she didn't even notice I wore the same clothes as the night before, but she made sure to inspect the beverage I sipped on. And it was then that she informed me I had reached the limit of sweets I was allowed for the day and wouldn't get any dessert at dinner unless I went on a five-mile run or spent an hour sweating the calories off at the gym, which I declined. There was nothing wrong with my figure. She just couldn't accept the fact that I didn't inherit her skinny genes and willingness to live on lettuce.

I stole a batch of freshly baked cookies from the kitchen and stuffed them in my pocket when I crossed paths with my mother again. It was time for her cucumber-infused water, her daily afternoon regimen. One she stopped forcing upon me a few years ago after I threw up the concoction all over her favorite rug.

In my bedroom, I admired my hair in the wall-length mirror, gathering it into a makeshift ponytail. I had no idea what to do with it. Dye it again, cut it short, or let it grow.

I took my time to shower and heard voices coming from downstairs. Curious, I put on one of my vintage band T-shirts and a pair of light gray baggy sweatpants, drying my wet hair with a towel. Deep down, I hoped Mom would be too busy with whatever she was doing and wouldn't notice how I dressed so I could wear this to dinner. Just a little act of rebellion that would be *so* satisfying.

If I discarded the sweatpants, turned the T-shirt into a dress, and added a belt and the ankle boots I got at the thrift store last weekend along with a few bracelets, it'd look great. If only… I sighed, my shoulders sagging. A girl was allowed to dream.

One voice amongst the others in the foyer caught my attention, and I stopped mid-stairs. No. *No, no, no.* It couldn't be, could it? I had to be dreaming. Or hallucinating. Dropping the towel, I locked eyes with a guy a little older than me. Blond messy hair, hazel eyes, chin dimple, and almost six feet tall, he looked as hot as he did the last time I saw him. His presence couldn't be a coincidence. All the air left my lungs at the thought. Okay, this had to be a bad joke… Or some kind of prank.

Panic coiled around my heart.

What was I supposed to do now?

Chapter 3

Joe

Standing in the foyer of my father's mansion, I surveyed the space around me. Since he sold his company two years ago, my dad had turned into a freaking multi-millionaire. Not that there was anything wrong with that. I loved the title. One I myself aspired to reach one day. But now random women tried to attach themselves to his status. Dad couldn't care less about the wealth and all that came with it. He just spent it to realize some of his dreams while he could still enjoy them. A villa in the Caribbean, this house, three cars, a yacht. Nice things made affordable by millions of dollars.

The only thing in his plan that I didn't agree with was his girlfriend, Clarissa. She was a full-time job on her own. The woman had no shame. All she ever tried to do was to get my dad to spend more. On her. She was a viper, but my old man—for a reason I still couldn't decipher—loved her.

I was glad he was happy. I really was. He deserved it.

After my mother died when I was a kid, he had put all his energy into raising me and bringing the business he started from scratch to what it had become today. His needs, they had always come last.

I just wished he had dated a little more before tying himself to the first woman who'd gotten into his bed in years and moving her in with her kid.

I moved to New York full-time a few years ago when I started college, and I was still living there. The fact that I had gotten a job on Broadway after graduation meant I rarely came to Silverville anymore. My father had insisted on flying me here this weekend because he had big news to announce, and I was afraid of what it might be. With Clarissa in the picture, anything was possible. And if the offspring was half as intense as her mother, three days here would feel like an eternity. I wasn't in the mood to deal with a pretentious high schooler. Some days, I was glad I didn't live so close that I was pressured to come to Sunday dinner every week.

When I had parked in the driveway of my father's mansion and hauled myself out of the rental a few minutes ago, my dad had welcomed me with open arms, not knowing that I had spent my night at Dick's Hole and fucked Isla senseless instead of coming home early.

"I can't believe you're home, son. It's been too long. We missed you around here."

My free time these days was rare, and it saved me from having to fly here too often and watch my dad and Clarissa give each other googly eyes and whisper dirty sweet nothings.

"Well, when you're the new guy on a long-running, coveted Broadway show, you can't say no when they book your schedule."

He clapped my back before pulling me into a hug.

"Still. I've missed you, son. I'm glad you're here for a few days." He released me. "Your bedroom is ready for you. I'm so glad to have you home. This place is too big for me. What was I thinking when I purchased it?"

I chuckled. "I'm sure Clarissa doesn't complain."

"Nah. She's more than happy to have an entire floor dedicated to her. Her daughter is here. We can't wait for you two to meet."

"Huh, yeah. The kid?"

"Joe. She's seventeen. Not exactly what I'd call a kid. Be open-minded, please. She's nice. A bit shy, but she's a good girl with a bright future in front of her. She could learn a lot from you."

"I'm warning you. I'm not on babysitting duty."

My dad snickered. "Stop being a brat. If anyone, between the two of you, needed a babysitter in high school, it certainly would not be her."

We both turned around at the sound of high heels clicking on the tiled floor.

Seconds later, my dad's girlfriend neared us. "Ohmygod, look at you." She hugged me, and I stayed still, unsure of what to do. From over her shoulder, I watched my father grinning, so I wrapped my arms stiffly around Clarissa, giving her back a pat, making an effort. We broke apart, and she moved to my father's side. "We're so happy you're joining us tonight." She clasped her hands in front of her. "Our first family outing. Isn't this exciting? This deserves a celebration. We'll have some champagne later… the good stuff." She and my dad exchanged a heated gaze, and I looked away, feeling like a voyeur.

My eyes landed on the figure coming down the stairs.

A girl. A young girl. Dressed down in baggy sweatpants and an old white T-shirt, drying her hair with the towel in her hand.

She lifted her head, and all the air in my lungs was sucked out. Every molecule of oxygen left my body. Dizziness made my head spin. I tried to swallow, but my mouth felt like sandpaper.

We eyed each other, and her lips parted. Neither of us said a thing as we took each other in.

"Grace," Clarissa barked, her voice high-pitched. I reared my head back, and looked at the girl, then at the mother as she yelled, "What did I tell you earlier? When will you learn to act like a lady? Not only are you looking like a lazy cat, but you are also parading around this house dressed like a homeless person."

My dad kissed Clarissa's temple. "Give the girl a break. We were teenagers too once. She's a nice kid. Come on, let her be."

"Yeah, well, I was busy working fifty hours a week in Milan when I was her age, not wasting my time with insignificant details no one cares about."

The girl held my gaze, as if daring me to say something about our night together. The initial shock eased, and my brain began to process the whole situation.What Clarissa said seconds ago sent alarm bells to my conscience. *Grace.* Last night, she said her name was Isla.

Wow, the audacity.

She had played me. Lied to me. For hours.

Fury boiled inside me. I glared at her, ready to explode.

Reality had a sour taste.

I had fucked the daughter of my father's girlfriend last night. Not only had I fucked the *daughter*, but I had fucked a girl who was clearly not in college.

A rumble of disgust stirred in my stomach, and for a second, I thought I'd be sick.

The girl from the bar, the one I'd shared an instant connection with, the best kiss of my life, the hottest night of my existence, lived under the same roof as my father and was a fucking high schooler.

"You okay?" my father asked, breaking the staring contest between Isla—Grace or whatever her name was—and me. Had anything she told me last night been true?

Growing up, I often found myself in uncomfortable situations. Yeah, too often my dick led my actions when I became a horny teenager at fifteen, but this…this was a new low, even for me.

"Joe, this is Clarissa's daughter, Grace. Grace, this is my son, Joe. I hope you two get along. Why don't you drop your bag in your room and freshen up? We're leaving at six. I made a reservation at your favorite bistro in town." He wrapped his arms around me once more. "I'm glad you're home, son." He let go of me and grabbed Clarissa's hand, stopping her from berating her daughter. "Come on, let's give the kids time to get acquainted. There's something I wanna show you."

Picking up my bag, I climbed the steps two at a time, stopping in front of a stunned Grace. "You," I said through gritted teeth, my jaw hurting under the pressure. "Isla? Really? Was everything you told me last night a lie?"

Her face flushed.

"Anything you wanna say in your defense?" Could she feel the anger pouring out from me?

"What do you want me to say?" She rolled her eyes as if I were overreacting and being ridiculous. "Don't look so surprised, Joe. You had time to deal with it already."

"Are you kidding me right now?" My molars would turn to dust soon if I didn't relax my jaw. I clamped her elbow and pulled her upstairs. She said nothing as I motioned her into my bedroom and kicked the door shut behind us. "What were you thinking?"

She nibbled her bottom lip, avoiding my gaze. "Joe, I-

I'm sorry. It wasn't how it was supposed to go down. I thought we'd never see each other again…"

"Shit. Well, that plan of yours sucked balls."

For a second, I saw the girl she pretended to be the night before. "It wasn't a plan… I just… I just thought you were hot and nice. And I don't regret our night together. Like it or not, that's the truth. By the way, I won't tell my mom. Or your dad."

"You better not. This stays between us. For the rest of time."

Moisture welled up in her eyes, and a part of me—the one who fell under her spell last night—wished I could pull her into a hug, kiss her, and make it all go away. I hated seeing her upset. But I knew better now. How could I have been so stupid?

"Joe, we shared something real last night. Don't try to convince me we didn't or act as if it didn't mean anything to you too. That *I* didn't mean anything to you. For a few hours, all I wanted was to be someone else. I'm tired of being the odd one. All I craved was a reprieve from my own life. Yesterday, I-I got into an argument with my mother after dinner… She said things I would rather forget. Her words, they hurt me. I went to that bar to drink my sorrows. You were a nice surprise in my shitty night. You made me feel beautiful…and desired. So much that I forgot I was sad. For what it's worth, I really did like you. A lot."

A tug-of-war raged inside me.

The whole situation was so confusing.

I let go of her and paced the room, about to rip my hair out, trying to calm down. "I fucked a kid. I slept with the daughter of my dad's plastic girlfriend." I sprang around, pointing an accusing finger at her. "How old are you? No bullshit. No lie." I threw my arms over my head.

My father said she was seventeen earlier, but I needed to hear the truth from her. "Your name is not even Isla, for God's sake."

Grace swallowed, tucking her hair behind her ear, a sheepish look painting her face. "I'll be eighteen soon. In… huh…December. I didn't lie about my birthday. I'm a Christmas baby."

"Whoa. No matter what you say, you lied about your age. Big time. You tricked me."

"No, I didn't."

"Yes, you did." Was she acting stupid on purpose?

"No. You were a stranger, so why would I have given you information about me? I'm not stupid. And for the record, you were the one who kissed me first, remember?"

"You were chugging booze in a bar. I asked you twice if you were old enough to drink. You said you were. Want me to refresh your memory? You also said you were taking some time off from school. I asked you if you were in college for God's sake."

She knotted her fingers together, glancing down. "It wasn't a lie. I-I just omitted to specify that it was high school."

"How could I have been so clueless? And I wasn't even that drunk when we met." I breathed through my nose. "Girl. You're such a piece of work. I knew it."

She crossed her arms over her chest, one hip jutting forward, defiance sparking in her eyes. "Takes one to know one."

"What does that mean?"

"Don't look so righteous, Joe. I've heard stories about you, you know. People talk. I've been living here for, what, two months? And so far, I've already learned fun stuff about your *sexcapades*. Don't act like you're above me. My classmates keep asking me if I'm the sister of *the* fuckboy.

And you graduated that high school years ago. Want me to explain it to you? Or to refresh *your* memory? The principal's daughter you banged in her office in senior year… Does the name Lizzy Cantrell ring a bell? You're pretty famous at Redmond Academy."

I shook my head. "Okay. Fine. I never claimed I was a monk. Told you I wasn't always a gentleman but never a jerk. The point is, I didn't lie. And my high school sexual encounters have nothing to do with the current situation." Once again, reality hit me like a cold shower. "I slept with a minor. Not only a minor, but also a girl almost six years younger than me. That's sick… *I'm* sick. Something is definitely wrong with me."

Grace stepped forward, putting a stop to my pacing with a hand splayed over my chest.

I flinched under her touch, but she didn't remove her hand.

Soon, my heart rate decreased at her contact, and I breathed easier as my body recognized her, and my mind realized I couldn't undo our night together.

"Joe, look at me. Age is not important here. What we shared last night wasn't a lie. It was real."

"Well, it matters to me."

"In my defense, I had no idea who you were. I swear. How was I supposed to know you were Phil's son? It's not like we shared IDs or something."

This house was a freaking museum. How could she have known? It wasn't like my face was plastered all over the place. The only framed picture my dad had of me was on his desk in his office, and I must have been twelve.

She cradled my cheek with her small hand, and for a beat, I forgot the girl in front of me was seventeen and forbidden, relaxing against her touch. The one still branded on my skin all these hours later. Yep, I was a sick bastard. No doubt.

"We can't," I whispered.

"I know. It felt amazing to live a life where I could be who I wished to be, though. Last night, I didn't trick you. I swear."

I quirked one brow.

"Okay, I lied about my age. It's a small detail."

"No. It's a big one. I feel like a creep. You had no right to pretend to be eighteen when you're not. It's not cool. And I could get arrested for that."

She bobbed her head twice. When she looked at me, I could read the defeat in her eyes. They glimmered with tears. "I'm… I'm sorry. I never thought we'd meet again. Or else I wouldn't have dragged you into my stuff." She paused. "I'm going through some…some things. As you may have noticed, being my mother's child isn't an easy feat. It comes with a lot of shaming. My world isn't as pretty and shimmery as it looks."

She spun on her heels and left my bedroom, taking all the viable oxygen in the room with her. I suffocated as I landed on my bed, pressing my hands against my skull, hoping the last ten minutes of my existence had been a nightmare that I would wake up from.

Unable to wrap my head around how the last twenty-four hours of my life had played out and my biggest screw-up in forever, I dialed my best friend. With the music deal he'd just signed, the guy had been super busy lately. Even though we didn't see each other as often as we did back when we were roommates in college, he was still one of my favorite people.

"Man, I was about to call you," Anderson greeted me. "You'll never guess who I bumped into today. I'm still shaking. This entire thing is a clusterfuck." I could hear the emotions lacing his voice.

"Well, you'll never guess what I did," I said, cringing at the memory of the previous night.

"Abby," Andy said at the same time I said, "I fucked a high school girl who turned out to be the daughter of my father's girlfriend."

"Shut up," we both said at the same time.

"Abby?" I asked, my eyes widening at the piece of information. "*Your* Abby? The one who got away and you spent months pining over? *That* Abby?"

"Yep. The one and only. She's my dad's new assistant. She dropped a bomb on me, but I won't say more until I have had time to talk with her about it." He paused. "You slept with a teenager? Were you drunk, or were you born stupid?"

I sighed. "Both. For my defense, I didn't know it was her... She pretended to be someone else. A college-aged someone else. I fell for it. It was the single most amazing night of my life. We connected. It wasn't just physical. I can't explain it. Anyway, hours later, when I drove to my father's mansion, I came face to face with the girl who disappeared from my bed earlier this morning. Can you imagine how bad this is?"

"Wow, I wouldn't wish to be you right now."

I facepalmed. "What am I supposed to do? Pretend we never met and that she never orgasmed around my fingers. Shit. From now on, every time I look at her, that's all I'm gonna remember."

"Lucky for you, you two don't live under the same roof. And it's not like your parents are married. Your dad might get tired of Clarissa and kick her out."

"Easier said than done. He moved them across the country. He's happy, man. I swear. I haven't noticed those glints in his eyes in a long time." I checked the time. "We should meet soon. I miss you, man. It's been too long since we last saw each other. You have to tell me more about what's going on with Abby. I still can't believe you found her after all this time. How small is this world?"

"Actually, my dad found her…but anyway, destiny is playing us. Big. Fucking. Time. To hear what I have to say, we'll need a lot of booze," Andy said. "I'm telling you, it's big. I need to come to terms with the fact first. Then I'll share everything."

"Good luck. I'm here whenever you need me. Gotta go. We have a family dinner."

"You're kidding, right?"

"I wish."

"It sucks being you. Let me know how it goes."

I scoffed. "Yeah. Sure. I'll spend the evening with a girl who's forbidden and who tricked me. One I fucked senseless for hours last night. I can't wait for the next three days of my life."

Chapter 4
Grace

Joe drove one of his father's cars to dinner while I was forced to sit in the backseat of Philip's SUV, listening to my mother talk about insipid topics no sane person would ever care about. During the entire ride, Philip kept her hand nestled in his, lifting it to his mouth to kiss her knuckles every now and then.

My mother looked at him with stars in her eyes, and I wondered if she really liked the guy or if she was pretending, the same way she'd done with all her ex-boyfriends. There had been a lot of them. Like a *lot*. A plastic surgeon —hello, fake boobs and nose job —a hotel owner, two dentists, and a sales rep for a pharmaceutical company amongst a dozen others.

Philip murmured something and kissed the side of her head. My mother shone beside him, and I hoped, for everyone's sake, she wasn't leading him on. So far, Philip had been kind to me, always taking my side whenever my mother chastised me over the smallest things. Honestly, it would kinda suck if we had to leave. In many ways, I loved having a father figure around, even though I still had to make friends in this town.

Most times, I was all alone in the castle. All my real friends lived far away—or rather, a few states away, and my boyfriend had broken up with me last summer after he learned I was moving to Pennsylvania. Dick.

Redmond Academy, that new private school Philip enrolled me in... well, let's just say I didn't fit in. Most students were gifted in something academic. Arts. Music. Technologies. Sciences. And they all came from money. I had no gift. Unless you considered transforming vintage clothes into fashion trends and styling hair, I was fairly basic compared to my peers. Oh, and I was a champion at getting under my mother's skin. That was one subject I was really skilled at.

All of this explained why I couldn't wait to move out, be in college, and start over. Far from everything I'd always known. Blank slate.

Perfect for a rebel like me.

"Did Joe and you find time to get acquainted earlier?" Philip asked, meeting my eyes through the rearview mirror.

I pinched my lips together to avoid spilling the truth that was dancing on the tip of my tongue. "Yep. All good."

"Awesome. I had a feeling you two would hit it off."

"Getting along just fine." If only he knew his son's hand had been inside my panties mere hours ago when I begged him to fuck me, he would have a heart attack.

For the rest of the drive, I blocked my mother and Philip's voices out, my attention solely on the scenery passing through the window.

Joe waited for us inside the restaurant, flirting with the hostess, a girl with mile-long legs, a tiny but perky chest, and a symmetric face with big doe eyes and pouty lips. Everything my mom wished I looked like. And everything I wasn't. Great.

"See?" Mom said, nudging my side. "That girl is putting time into her appearance. And it works… Look. Joe is probably about to ask for her number." She exhaled. "If only you could put some effort and shed a few pounds, you'd be less miserable. Popular and beautiful girls are never alone." She turned and locked arms with Philip, who was oblivious to the under-the-breath jabs and judgment my mom threw at me every chance she got.

In the wide mirror behind the bench that served as the waiting area, I gave myself a slow once-over. Sure, my hips were wider than the hostess's, and my arms and legs were not as skinny as hers, but I loved my appearance. My full breasts, my high cheekbones, and natural, thick lashes. The royal blue dress I was wearing—the band T-shirt I'd transformed into a dress didn't make the cut—landed mid-thighs and accentuated my cleavage and my waist. I smiled at my reflection. My mom could say anything she wanted; I was trying really hard not to let her words play with my insecurities. Most days it was difficult, and I inspected each inch of my body in the mirror when I dressed up in the morning. I was there when she pinched my thighs in kindergarten and said I was destined to have cellulite growing up. What a thing to say to a kid. I never wanted to end up like her. I had seen her throwing up on purpose when I was just a little kid because she thought the dinner she ate would live in her ass forever. My mother's mind was filled with fashion fads and body shaming. She not only body-shamed and criticized me, but she did the same to herself. I'd witnessed the dozens of diets she tried over the years, all in the name of a perfect body—or what she considered perfection. Some left her with thinning hair, others with decaying teeth.

She never found joy or peace, despite the torture she put her body and mind through. I refused to be a victim of her sickness. No normal human being should live like she did for the sake of it. She'd likely gone all day without eating, just to prepare for tonight. And she'd punish herself for this by spending hours sweating at the gym all week.

A gentle touch on the small of my back snapped me out of my trip down memory lane. When I cocked my head, Joe stood next to me, almost too close for comfort. "Are you ready? They're waiting for us. Your mom called your name twice."

I stared at him, trying to process his words, escaping the thoughts that had overtaken my brain.

"Are you okay?" he asked.

I bobbed my head. "Yeah…huh…sure. Just got lost in my mind for a second."

His cheek grazed mine when he spoke into my ear. "By the way, you're looking fucking hot tonight. Stop trying to impress me. It won't work. I'm not playing your games anymore. Stay away from me." He adjusted the cuffs of his black dress shirt and kept his smile anchored to his handsome face as if he'd just complimented me. In a way, he had.

We all followed the hostess to our table. The restaurant combined chic elegance with rustic charm. I was certain it wasn't my mother's choice. Black carpeted floor, square tables covered with red tablecloths, and leather chairs. Besides the few wall-mounted lights, the room was lit by candles flickering on each table. Quite romantic. Classical music played in the background. Not what I expected for our first "family" dinner—quote marks required.

Philip sat by my mom, which forced me to sit next to

Joe. Why couldn't we all sit on a different side of the table? The last thing I wished for was to have him in my personal space all night.

"Joe used to play here every weekend when he was still in high school," Philip said, pointing to the grand piano in one corner of the room. "It has always been one of our favorite restaurants."

"Oh, I forgot you're trained in classical music," my mother said. "I adore Frédéric Chopin."

I snorted, and she murdered me with her eyes. My mother knew nothing about music. She was just trying to look interested…and interesting. I was certain she'd looked up 'Best pianists of all time' online before coming here, hoping to sound smarter than she actually was.

The server brought us a bottle of champagne, and Philip nodded when the server showed it to him first for approval. He popped the cork and poured the champagne into four crystal flutes.

Philip raised his glass. "I'm so happy we're all together because tonight, we're celebrating."

Mom lifted her left hand and blurted out, "We're getting married," smiling like a fool. She wasn't a woman prone to showing her emotions too often, so it took me by surprise when her eyes brimmed with tears, and she fanned herself with her hand.

Beside me, Joe stiffened.

My mouth hung half-open, like a startled fish, and all the thoughts mixed together in my head.

"Isn't it wonderful?" my mother exclaimed. "The four of us will be family. Officially."

Time stood still. We all stared at one another, but nobody said anything.

"Aren't you guys going to say something?" Philip asked.

"Wow," was Joe's only reply.

I tried to appear more enthusiastic. "Great. When's the wedding?"

"End of November," my mother said. "I know it's in five weeks, but we couldn't wait." She stared at her future husband as if he had hung the moon for her. "We love each other so much."

Philip took her hand in his and brought it to his lips, kissing her knuckles just like he had done in the car earlier.

Without another word, Joe pushed his chair back, threw his balled napkin on the table, and excused himself. "I'll be right back," he called over his shoulder, padding toward the bar area.

"I can't wait to see you wear the maid of honor gown I chose for you, Grace. You'll look fabulous, you'll see."

"She always looks fabulous," Philip chimed in.

I offered him a hint of a smile as a thank you.

While our parents got lost in their own love bubble, I surveyed the restaurant for the one person who could understand how I felt but had vanished almost twenty minutes ago. No sign of him anywhere.

I served myself another glass of champagne, and nobody seemed to care I'd be drunk by the end of the night if they didn't stop me.

Philip ordered a bunch of dishes to share and more champagne when he noticed the bottle was empty.

I kept drinking, trying to understand my mother's strategy. Was she really in love with Philip, or was he just another pawn in her game? So far, I couldn't tell for sure.

As predicted, Mom ate almost nothing while I fixed my plate with a little bit of everything.

The seat next to mine remained empty. At some point, I stood up, pretending to head to the ladies' room but actually planning to explore the restaurant and look for my new *stepbrother*. Just the word gave me the creeps.

The same hostess, who had greeted us when we arrived, met me when I rounded the corner. "I'm sorry to bother you, but your boyfriend is drunk at the bar. We'd like you to escort him outside. Customers are complaining." She pointed behind her with a thumb.

I stopped in my tracks. "Boyfriend?"

"Well, the guy you were with earlier."

"Oh, *that* boyfriend." I nodded as if it made sense.

"You have more than one boy in your life? If you do, I wouldn't get too attached to this one." She turned and walked away without another word. Whoa, blunt much. If I remembered correctly, she was the one flirting with him when I first got here.

Following her directions, I reached the bar section of the restaurant. Joe was at the back of the U-shaped counter, his tongue down another girl's throat, and cupping her ass with both hands while she rubbed herself against him.

I watched them, bile rising at the back of my throat at the sight. An tight knot tied my stomach. My palms became slick with sweat. I wasn't allowed to feel the pang of jealousy developing inside me. It was stupid…and unwelcome. And yet, it spread through me like wildfire.

Nearing the tonsils show playing in front of my eyes, I harrumphed, resting my fists on my hips.

Joe tilted his head, his glossy eyes boring into mine.

His were void of warmth, bloodshot and hooded. He looked nothing like the guy I fell for the night before. Gone was his easygoing charm and contagious smile. He appeared dejected. A sadistic curl bent his lips. "What do you want, *sis?*" His tone was mocking. At that moment, I wondered how I ever found him attractive.

"You're drunk, *brother.*"

"Wow, you're perceptive. Want an award for being a smartass?"

I inhaled and exhaled slowly. "The restaurant people asked me to get you out of here. It seems they don't like porn shows taking place in their establishment."

"Porn shows?" He echoed my words with disdain.

"Yeah. People don't appreciate your little display of… of whatever you're doing."

He laughed, jerking his head back. "That's not what she said last night. If I recall her exact words, they were *Fuck me.* Don't you feel like a fraud right now? When my dick slid into—"

I pushed the girl to the side, silencing Joe with a hand over his mouth. He wrapped his arms around my waist, and I melted a little against him. Until my conscience returned and I snapped out of it. "You," I told the girl, flicking my finger at her, "get lost. And you," I brought my focus on Joe, "I'm taking you home."

"Oh god, she's taking me home. It feels like a *déjà-vu.* In reverse." There was no humor in his laughter.

"Stop being a brat and let's go."

"I'm not done here." He called after the girl, "Don't go. She'll go."

I pushed his chest back with all my strength. "What are you doing? What are you trying to prove?"

He lifted his hands between us in defense. "I'm just trying to get rid of the taste of you. I've gotta fuck you out of my system, so please let me be and go play with your dolls elsewhere."

"My dolls?"

"Yep. Because you are a kid. A. Kid. In. High school. And I'm in my twenties. Do you need me to draw it for you? Because you can't read? Or perhaps you flunked math. How old are you again? Oh yes, too young. And it has nothing to do with good genes. Gosh, you had me there. I gave you the benefit of the doubt. You tricked me. Stabbed me in the heart and left me bleeding. One of the best nights of my life. And what did I gain in return? Lies. Fucking lies. And more lies. Oh, and a new *mom*. You two should gather all your stuff and go back to where you belong. Far from here. Pack your bags, and get the hell away from our lives. For good. Is it too hard to—"

"You want us gone? Do you think I wanted to come here? To be moved across the country before my senior year of high school and lose all my friends? The only home I've ever known? Do you think it's easy for me to attend a school filled with rich pricks who think they're better than me? And who talk about you like you're the Slut King of Silverville? No. You have no idea how it is for me. You live in fucking New York. You're only here for the weekend. After that, you're going back to your life. I'm the one who has to live under the same roof as our parents. I'm. The. One. Stuck. Here. So, I'm sorry for bothering your perfect little life, but you walked away from it a long time ago. Stop acting like an entitled *princess* and grow up. I thought you were twenty-three, not three."

"Stop thinking you're better than me. You're full of shit. That much is evident… Even from miles away. Also, hate to break it to you, but you've got daddy issues. I found out firsthand when you cornered me in that—"

A deep voice from behind startled us both. "Enough."

In slow motion, I turned around and came face to face with Philip.

A wave of heat filled my cheeks.

How much did he hear? Ohmygod, we were so screwed. *I* was so screwed. But I was a minor. If everything went to shit, it would be Joe who would take the blame for it all. I had no idea what the age of consent here in Pennsylvania was, but I couldn't let anything happen to him. After all, I was the one who lied to him. Who made him believe things that didn't exist.

"*Daaad*," Joe slurred, unable to hide how wasted he really was. "I…I was just telling *myyy* new *sister* that—"

"Philip, I can explain," I said, cutting him short, hoping he would hear me out.

He raised a hand in a commanding gesture I wasn't used to. My mother had never been good with discipline. Unless it concerned my physical appearance, she didn't really care about my actions. "Both of you, silence." Joe and I clamped our mouths shut. "Clarissa and I were excited to share the good news with you two. You are our children, and soon we'll all be one family. The last thing I thought would happen tonight was finding my son drunk off his ass and the two of you arguing on the day you met for the first time."

Joe lifted a hand. "Technically, it-it's not really"—he hiccupped—"the first…"

I blinked, afraid he would come clean to his father and mess up everything. Was he suicidal or something? Did he really think our parents would be fine with us having sex?

In what world was he living in? Did he have any idea how batshit my mother would become if she learned the truth?

Philip continued as if he didn't hear him, and I breathed a sigh of relief.

"You two go back home. Go to bed and sleep it off. We'll have a talk in the morning. For now, just get out of here. I'll call a cab for you."

Joe dangled the car keys. "I'll…I'll drive us home. *Nooo*

worries. I'll take care of my *baby sis* while I'm at it. Don't *worry*. I know exactly what she…" He closed his eyes for a second and massaged his temple with his fingers. "Oh *yeahhh*. I know exactly what she likes *annnd* how *shhhe* likes it." He winked at me, and I fought within me the urge to slap his handsome face.

His dad removed the keys from his grip, and after opening an app on his phone to book us a car, he followed us toward the entrance. "I'm disappointed in you, son. This was supposed to be our night. Clarissa's and mine. You should be ashamed… I know this whole wedding thing may look rushed to you guys, but Clarissa and I are happy, and you gotta respect that." He shook his head, his shoulders sagging in defeat. "I really wish you two could be friends, you know. You don't have to like each other, but please act civilized."

"I'm sorry," I murmured.

Joe pushed past me and exited the restaurant. Through the window, I could see him pacing the sidewalk, shaking his head, and cursing.

Philip's hand rested on my shoulder and gave it a squeeze. "He'll be all right. He didn't mean what he said earlier. I don't know what's got into him. He's been different for the last couple of months. Alone and sad. He won't confide in me, but I sense a change in him. That's why I wanted him to spend the weekend here. To decompress. He's working too much. Soon, he'll burn out if he doesn't take care of himself. I wish he would talk to me. Don't let him intimidate you with words, okay? Inside, he's a softie. He just puts on a brave face to hide his pain. His mother's death affected him more than he'll ever admit. He started acting out after that day…" A chime on his phone had Philip unlocking the device. "Your car will be here in a minute. I should go back to your mother. Just make sure you both get home safe, okay? I'll see you two in the morning."

With one last glance at his son, Philip retreated to the dining room, waving at my mother as he neared her.

I forced myself to look away and joined my future *step-brother* outside.

For the entire ride home, Joe and I sat on opposite ends of the backseat, not engaging with each other.

When we entered the house, he turned to face me. His words sounded like venom and spread under my skin, poisoning all my vital organs. "*Whaaat* happened between us was a mistake. I…I was drunk; otherwise, I would have *nevvver* fallen for a girl like *youuu*. You're pathetic. A manipulator *annnd* a liar. I-I'm sorry we gotta see each other again in the *forseale*…no…foreseeable future. I wish we'd *nevvver* met. Stay the *fuckkk* away from me. Don't talk to *meee*…huh…don't reach out, don't look at *meee*. Did I…Did I make myself clear?"

I nodded as hot tears rolled down my cheeks. Joe's words hurt more than any of the mean things my mother ever said to me. They infiltrated my heart and blanketed it with darkness.

I knew the night we shared was a mistake, yet the time we spent together still surpassed every other night of my life. It meant something to me. It felt real.

I swallowed the lump clogging my airways.

Joe stood there, glaring at me. I felt small under the intensity of his murderous gaze.

"I-I didn't just *fuckkk* the underaged daughter of my dad's girlfriend last night. I fucked *myyy* new *little sister*. And…and I liked it so much that all day, before I-I bumped into *youuu* and learned the truth, I had hoped for a…for a repeat. *Youuu're* toxic, and you mean nothing to me. I-I'm done with *youuu*."

He turned around and climbed the stairs toward his bedroom two at a time, leaving me behind.

I rubbed my arms with my hands, trying to inject myself with warmth. Because Joe only left iciness in his wake.

Chapter 5

Joe

"I can't believe your dad is getting married," Anderson said, adjusting his bowtie in the mirror of my en-suite bathroom. I got back to my dad's house early this morning. It had been five weeks since the weekend I would rather erase from my memory when I ran away in the morning after Grace and I got into a fight. A stupid fight, but I had to blow off steam and get the angst out in any possible way. Even after all this time, I couldn't wrap my head around the fact I had slept with her a few hours before learning we were about to be related.

This time around, I begged Andy to act like a buffer between me and the rest of my new family. My dad loved him, so it shouldn't be hard. When we were in college, my father hired him every year to play at his company's Christmas party. Back when he wasn't on the way to becoming an international superstar. The past few weeks had been a real challenge for him since she reappeared in his life out of nowhere. He had his own shit to deal with, but I was thankful he took a day off to help me out. And anyway, I was pretty sure my father asked him to play today as a favor too.

"Yeah, well, if he's happy, who am I to interfere, right?"

"Any hot encounter with your sister?" my friend asked. "I still can't believe you two had dirty sex. If you would keep it in your pants sometimes, stuff like this wouldn't happen to you."

"Said the guy who was hung up on his one-night stand for years."

He lifted in arms in defense. "At least we're not about to become siblings."

"Half-siblings."

"Your dad should adopt her. You would all share the same last name. *The Crawfords.* Perfect happy little family. The dream."

I punched his side. "If you don't shut it up, I'll kick your ass out of here."

My friend quirked a brow. "And who's going to save your stupid self if I'm gone?"

"Fine. You can stay." I sighed. "The last time I saw her, I said terrible things to her. I was drunk, so the memory is a bit hazy, but I'm pretty sure I made her cry."

"Fuck. You're an insensitive bastard sometimes. Okay, she lied to you about her age, but she couldn't guess you were Phil's son. Maybe, for her too, it was a memorable night."

"Not interested to know anymore. I gotta move on and forget about that little incident… Anyway, how are you doing? Seriously. I know the bomb Abby dropped on you changed all your professional plans."

He scratched his nape, avoiding my eyes. "One day at a

time. The last time I saw her, we had a huge fight... It's hard to immerse myself in her routine. She doesn't always make it easy on me. Even though we don't always agree, somehow, when things are running smoothly, I'm falling harder than I ever thought I could. The reality shook me to the core, but I've never been happier. Even when she keeps me at arm's length..."

I clapped his shoulder. "I'm glad. You really deserve to thrive in everything you do, man. After everything your parents put you through, this is the happy ending you worked all your life for."

"Thanks, man." He checked the time on his phone. "Ready? The ceremony is starting in less than an hour, and I gotta get settled. My guitar case is still in my truck. I'll grab it and meet you in the garden."

My father had rented a big, heated white tent that had been pitched in the backyard. November was cold and snowy here in Pennsylvania, but the wedding planner had come up with a set-up that would mimic a summer wedding—with a winter theme.

Silver and white bows covered the backrests of the chairs.

Soft music played on the speakers that had been mounted in the corners of the tent.

A wall made of white flowers and silver pearls adorned the back of the altar.

Even though I wasn't excited about this wedding, I had to admit it looked magical. Like a snow globe. And very wintery without being too much.

Winter Wonderland as my dad described it to me when we talked about it.

Today, we wore matching pearl gray suits, vests over white shirts, and red ties.

Mason Pierce, one of my cousins who lived out of state

with his wife, joined me by the makeshift bar as I grabbed bottles of water to take to Anderson. "How is it going, man?" he asked when I handed him one. "Long time no see."

"Good. How are you doing?"

He cast a glance down. "Better."

"The day of the funeral…you looked…huh…out of it. I'm sorry I left without saying goodbye. I had no idea what to say. My heart broke for you guys. I just—"

"It's okay. We all react differently to death."

"How's Melinda doing?"

"Good. She's taking care of Ride. His presence in our lives is God-sent. We have a purpose, someone who needs us. It helps to focus on what we *can* control."

"I'm glad it's working out. We should get together sometimes."

Mason was about fifteen years older than me, and growing up, I had always looked up to him. He was the big brother I never had.

My phone chimed with a notification. "Give me a sec," I told my cousin.

UNKNOWN:

9-1-1

Before I had time to reply, another message came through.

UNKNOWN:

It's Grace, by the way.

Anger pooled in my belly. How did she get my number? I thought I told her to forget about me the last time we talked. Sure, I knew we'd bump into each other at some point today, but I had planned on keeping as much distance between us as humanly possible.

ME:

Forget I exist. I thought I had been clear the last time.

UNKNOWN:

I need your help. I wouldn't ask if there was anyone else I could text.

Please.

ME:

Why?

UNKNOWN:

It's humiliating enough. Don't ask for a picture.

ME:

Is it another one of your tricks?

UNKNOWN:

Joe. Please. A girl needs help... I need help. Now. Or I'll be late for our parents' wedding.

ME:

Fine. Where are you?

UNKNOWN:

My bedroom. Hurry.

I returned my attention to my cousin. "Sorry, man. Something came up. Can we talk later?"

"Sure. Go." He dismissed me with a wave of his hand.

As I rushed toward the house, I wondered what Grace wanted help with. Deep down I hoped it wouldn't be an orgasm. With her, nothing seemed too far-fetched.

The door of her bedroom opened before I could knock.

"What the... What did you do?" I asked, blinking at the scene unfolding in front of me.

"Shut up and help me out. I'm suffocating, and it's gonna rip if you don't remove it off me."

Grace was stuck in her maid of honor gown. And when I said stuck, I wasn't kidding. The fabric was strained and ballooned into a mess around her body. From where I stood, I had the perfect view of her creamy thighs and white panties. Layers of red and light gray tulle and taffeta went in all directions, and she had one arm hanging by her side and the other, straight in the air above her head as if she had tried to put the gown on and got attacked by it instead.

"How am I supposed to help you out of it?"

"No idea. But we have less than an hour to fix this disaster."

"Did you know there's usually a zipper on the side, and it makes it easier to put on?" I knew because my mother used to wear a lot of gowns when she attended charitable events, and I was always the one zipping her up while Dad was busy getting ready himself. It's ironic how the woman who dedicated all her free time to breast cancer research ended up being taken by the same illness.

"I'm not some dumb bimbo. My mother. She chose the wrong size—like she always does—and then insisted I lose ten pounds to fit into it."

"She what? Care to repeat that?"

"She asked me to lose weight. Even got me those pills. I refused to take them or to sweat my life on a treadmill. Didn't lose any weight and now I gotta fit into a dress that's two sizes smaller than what I usually wear."

I stood there, my jaw hanging open, unable to speak. I'd always known Clarissa was kind of lunatic, but that? That took it to a whole new level.

"And she's been doing this since?"

She shrugged. "All my life. She gets angry because the

gap between my thighs is not wide enough or my waist isn't small enough. I'm never pretty enough or tall enough or slim enough. Whatever I do, it's never good enough for her."

Her eyes shimmered with unshed tears, and I hated my future stepmother with every ounce of my being.

"Grace, you are beautiful. I swear. I noticed it the first time I laid eyes on you. I-I couldn't look elsewhere… There's just something about you. A magnetism. I could tell that night someone had hurt you. I just never thought *that* someone would turn out to be your mother and that she would bully you about your appearance."

"You don't mean it…" She sniffled. "Don't try to be nice to me because you think it's what I wanna hear."

"I'm not."

She shook her head. "Most times, I succeed in creating a wall between my mother's words and my heart. I started doing this a long time ago… I…I love myself…or I used to. These days, I'm not so sure I like the girl who looks back at me in the mirror in the morning. All I see are the imperfections my mom keeps pointing at. Some days are harder than others."

"Fuck." What else could I say? Clarissa didn't deserve to be a mother. How could she hurt her own kid on purpose? The thought repulsed me. With a hand, I motioned Grace over. "Come here. I'll help you out."

She inched closer, and I pushed my hands under the layers of fabric, my palms gliding over her soft flesh. Goose bumps woke up all over her skin under my touch. Memories from our night together played back on a loop in my mind. Even though I had tried to erase every detail from my brain, I could remember each minute with clear precision.

Tension swirled inside me, straining my upper back.

Careful not to rip the fabric and strangle Grace, I peeled the gown off her inch by inch until I could set her free. When she turned to face me, a river streamed down her cheeks, messing with my composure—and my heart. She appeared so fragile right now. A far cry from the assertive girl I met that night in the bar or the one I fought with the last time I was in town. Her armor had vanished, leaving her defenseless.

The caring side of me took over, and I pulled her into my arms, cradling the back of her head with one hand as she cried into my shirt, her half-naked body pressed against mine, my other hand resting between her shoulder blades.

"Shhh, it's going to be all right. Please, don't cry."

She sobbed harder.

"What did I say? I'm just trying to comfort you here. Tell me what do to."

"I-I have nothing to…to wear. My mother is getting married, and I'm…and I'm gonna walk down the aisle next to her naked."

A soft laugh escaped despite myself. "You won't be naked."

Grace punched my chest. "Not funny. My makeup is ruined, my hair is probably a mess by now, and I'm too fat to fit into that gown."

"Never say again you're fat. I won't allow it because it's a lie, and I already warned you about lying to me."

"Stop. Why would *you* care? You hate me, remember?" Her sobs doubled in intensity. "Don't…don't pretend you're on my team. Not after all the hurtful things you said to me the last time we talked."

"I didn't really mean them. I was mad at you. You got under my skin, and what I thought was the greatest night of my life turned out to be a tainted memory. I was…hurt. And acted like a selfish prick."

"I don't believe you."

Holding her upper arms, I leaned back to look at her, and more pieces of my heart shattered at the sight. With a gentle touch, I dried her tear-soaked cheeks with the pad of my thumb. "I'm here, aren't I? I'm sure we can find a solution. Together."

Chapter 6

Grace

Thanks to my sewing abilities and creativity, I got to work and managed to transform my maid of honor gown in record time with the help of my stepbrother-to-be. When we put our differences aside, we made a pretty great team.

I kept the skirt part of the gown, and Joe offered me his jacket to wear as a top. It drew full attention to my cleavage. I accessorized the makeshift dress with a wide belt. Beside me, Joe rolled up the sleeves of his button-up shirt, adjusted his vest, and fixed his red tie. With his blond hair combed to the side and gelled in place, he looked very handsome. But still forbidden. No matter how many times I had dreamed about his hands on me and the softness of his lips at night when the lights were off and my imagination took over.

Once I fixed my hair and makeup, I spun on myself in

front of the mirror, admiring the final result. "How do I look?"

"Fucking gorgeous with a side of rebel," Joe said. "I love you in my clothes." As if he realized what he just said, he clamped his mouth shut. "Huh… I mean, you did a great job here. You should be proud of yourself. You have incredible talent."

"Thanks. I'm kinda proud. Let's see if I live long enough to enjoy it."

Joe pulled me to him and planted a kiss on the top of my head. "I'll make sure she stays the fuck away from you. And once this wedding is over, Clarissa will hear from me."

"No. Please. She'll take it out on me. If I survive tonight, I'll lie low for a while until she gets over it. It usually does the trick."

"Bab—" He coughed to silence his own words. "Grace." It sounded like a warning. "That's not the way to live, and you deserve better from your own mother than being chastised for being beautiful. I swear, she's just jealous."

"Impossible. She was the queen of the runway back in her day."

"I bet she was miserable. Always watching what she ate, having people criticizing her body all the time, not being able to enjoy pizza without being shamed for it. You are you. From what I've seen of you so far, you're unapologetic and assertive. If I were her, I'd envy you too."

"Thanks. Even though it's not the truth, I love everything you just said." I grabbed his hand between both of mine, needing his confidence to bleed on me. "We gotta go, or they'll start without us." I turned to fully face him. "Thanks for rescuing me earlier. I don't wanna fight with you, okay? I never had a big brother before, and I always imagined how much fun it would be to hang out with him if I had one." I rose on my tiptoes and kissed his lips. "For what could have been," I whispered. "In a few minutes, we'll never be able to do this ever again."

Tugging me against his hard chest, Joe kissed me back. A last-chance, toe-curling kiss. My mouth tilted up when he stepped back, and with my thumb, I wiped the lipstick smudge across his bottom lip.

"There. Let's go."

Joe intertwined our fingers and led me downstairs.

To avoid a nuclear war, I stayed clear of my mother until the wedding planner came to get me, my cue to walk down the aisle. I heard my mother's curse from behind me when she no doubt saw what I was wearing. I didn't care. The entire time, my focus stayed on Joe, looking too hot for his own good, as he stood beside his father. He winked, and I felt a blush creeping up my cheeks. I tried to keep my face neutral but failed at reeling in the grin that threatened to break free on my face.

The princess side of me had pictured a day like this once, sometime in the future. Me in a white gown, my prince waiting for me with glints in his eyes.

That prince wouldn't have tousled blond hair and hazel eyes. But I prayed he would look at me the way Joe did right now. Watching me like he craved to devour me. Our relationship, though, would always be—unlike mine with Joe—simple. We wouldn't have to hide our attraction or feel like we ever did something wrong by getting together. I'd be happy. And free.

A tiny part of my heart wished Joe could have been that prince. And yet, being attracted to your step-siblings felt every shade of wrong. But here I was. And having sex with them was another level of fucked-up. And here I was, having done exactly that. Even though we would never be related by blood, Joe and I were still about to become family.

That sealed the deal, no matter what my heart thought of the whole situation.

I reached the altar, and Joe stepped forward, offering me his arm as he escorted me to my spot on the opposite side, facing him. Seconds later, Philip offered my mother his arm and guided her to stand across from him at the altar.

She glanced at me over her shoulder, an accusing glare in her eyes, before shaking her head and bringing her attention back to her husband-to-be. I breathed easier once I met Joe's eyes, and he nodded. Yes, we were in this together. He would have my back.

The ceremony passed in a blur.

The newlyweds exchanged vows and kissed, and people applauded.

Joe and I linked arms as we walked down the aisle, followed by our parents. A guy with a soulful voice sang about love and magic while playing his guitar.

A server offered us glasses of pink champagne, and our parents got swallowed by the wave of guests raving about the bride's dress, how cute they looked together, the winter-inspired decor, and the choice of music.

"Grace, this is my best friend, Anderson Ford," Joe introduced me to the guy with the guitar.

Anderson extended his hand for me to shake. "Call me Andy. It's nice to finally meet the girl who succeeded at fucking with Joe's mind without even trying. I never thought I'd see the day when someone would put his heart through the wringer."

I elbowed Joe's ribs. "You begged me not to say anything to anyone, but you told your friend. Nice."

"C'mon. It's Andy. Sometimes, a guy needs to get his

ass kicked by his best friend when he can't do it on his own."

I rolled my eyes. "Whatever. You asked me to keep it a secret and I did. I expected the same decency from you."

"Girl, you did a number on him," Anderson chimed in.

"Just for the record, it was never my intention."

"Same result. Please be gentle with his heart. Before you happened, we all thought he didn't possess one."

"It's not mine to care for," I added. "Joe is a big boy. He can do it all by himself."

Anderson leaned toward a speechless Joe. "Sassy. Now I get it."

Joe punched his shoulder. "Shut up, man."

His friend chuckled. "And yet you spent countless hours telling me I should move on after Abby. How do you like being served the same medicine? Karma, man. I swear, you deserve every minute of your punishment."

"It's not the same." Joe's clamped his nape with one hand, looking anywhere but at us.

"It's not for you to decide, man. I think you hit the jackpot here."

I couldn't follow their conversation anymore. Some insider joke I wasn't part of. "Go ahead, keep arguing. I'll leave you to it and grab some food. I'll meet you two later."

I saw my mother laughing with her now-husband further on my right, so I veered left, reaching the bar in just a few strides.

I was nibbling on finger food when the air tensed around me. Without having to turn around, I could sense my mother standing behind me. From her hastening breaths, I knew she was pissed. Plastering a smile on, I pivoted until we faced each other.

"Mom. You look beautiful." I chewed on a piece of

cheese, trying to act as nonchalant as I could muster. "Want me to grab you champagne?"

If looks could kill, my mother would burn me alive. "Grace. What did you do to your dress? You… You… I can't even find the words to tell you how furious I am with you right now. Is this some rebellious act because you crave attention, or are you out of your mind? Joe was supposed to match with Philip, and you and I were supposed to match. You disrespected both of us by destroying the gown I chose for you."

"Mom." I inhaled. How could I make her understand? "It was too tight. I couldn't slip it over my head. I…I got stuck."

Madness shaped her lips. "I don't know what to do with you anymore, Grace. I'm tired of your acts of defiance. What did I do to deserve you as a daughter? Life would be much simpler if you were to listen to me once in a while. You had to ruin your gown. If you had taken the pills I bought for you and counted your calories like I instructed you to, we wouldn't be fighting about it right now."

"Mom. Stop. Do you hear yourself? Can't you love me for me? The gown didn't fit, and I used my creativity and talent to fix it. I'm pretty pleased with the result. It looks fierce. And badass. Why can't you just accept me as I am? For once, can't you enjoy your night without trying to spoil mine? I will never look like you do, and I'm perfectly fine with it."

"Grace, I'm so ashamed. You had to steal my thunder, didn't you?"

"You think I craved the attention on me? On your wedding day? Clearly, you know nothing about me. I'm glad you found Philip, and if you're happy, I'm happy for you. Is it too hard for you to accept?"

"You've never wanted me to be happy, Grace. All your life, you've disapproved of me and the men I've dated. Deep down, I think you envy me. You see how they all look at me, and you fear no one will ever give you the same attention."

I blinked. "Mom, you're delusional."

She let out an angry sneer. "Me? Delusional? One day, you'll thank me for teaching you how to take care of your body because it's the first thing people see when they look at you. Why would they wish to get to know you better when you can't do anything right?" She jabbed an accusing finger at my face. "Your eyeliner is too thick. And your eyeshadow isn't applied properly. It makes your left eye appear bigger. Don't get me started on that cleavage of yours. Just because you think it's your greatest asset, it doesn't mean you gotta flaunt it for everyone else to see. And certainly not on my wedding day."

I could feel my resistance starting to crack. "Are you… are you serious?"

Her face turned an angry shade of red. "Do I look like I'm kidding? Is it all a big joke to you?"

I stayed mute as she kept complaining about the silliest details. Her poisonous words felt like a million tiny needles stabbing my heart.

I had no more fight left in me, and my shoulders dropped in defeat. "Mom, think whatever you want… I'm done trying to make you proud or earn your approval." Lifting my skirt with both hands to avoid tumbling, I ran away, unable to stop the flow of tears rolling down my cheeks.

I didn't have to endure my mother's treatment any longer. In less than a month, I'd be eighteen and free of her.

I kicked my heels off as soon as I entered the house,

hurrying up the stairs leading to my bedroom. I fetched a suitcase from the walk-in closet and packed a bunch of clothes, not taking the time to check if they matched or were practical. My tears blinded my vision. My heart cracked in my chest. I had to get away from here. To disappear.

I removed the pins holding my hair, letting the blonde curls—that took an hour to perfect earlier—down and removed as much of my makeup as I could with a warm washcloth.

I was done pretending to be someone else for my mother's sake. I was done playing a part I had no interest in, and faking being happy I was falling apart inside.

I slipped my feet into a pair of sneakers and picked up my suitcase.

With heavy steps and an even heavier heart, I looked around and closed the door behind me before making my way downstairs toward Philip's garage.

"Grace, where are you going? I've been looking everywhere for you. My dad asked me to find you for the pictures before they serve dinner. Where are you going? Why-why do you have a suitcase?"

Joe's voice made me halt for a quick second before I resumed my run, not glancing at him.

"Grace? Wait up."

I refused to look at him—to let him see how broken I was inside. The faster I got out of here, the better it would be for everyone else, including myself.

I shouldered the garage door open, but before it clicked shut behind me, a strong hand looped around my waist and held me back, preventing me from escaping.

"Joe, let go of me."

His grip on me tightened. "No. Where are you going?"

"Away."

"But where?" Was it worry I could hear in his voice?

I shrugged. "Doesn't matter. If I leave, I won't be a burden to anyone anymore. My mom. You." My voice cracked. "It's better this way. Goodbye."

"Nope. Not that fast." Without letting go, he turned me around until he could look me in the eye. "Explain yourself."

In that instant, I wished the ground would open up beneath me and swallow me whole. "Please." My voice sounded foreign and helpless. Like my heart. "I gotta go." I refused to meet his eyes.

"No."

Why couldn't he mind his own business for once? I yanked my arm away, but he cradled my face with both hands, forcing my eyes to level with his. His voice sounded gentle. As if he was afraid to break me more than I already was. "You've been crying. You untied your hair and removed your makeup, and I'm certain you're about to commit a felony by stealing one of my dad's cars. Talk to me."

I forced hardness into my words. "Go ahead. Snitch on me. I don't care. I don't give a shit anymore." I grew walls around myself. Joe wouldn't gain access to my heart this time around. I was done taking bullshit from people who were supposed to love me and care about me.

His face twisted with some emotions I couldn't define, and when he leaned in, he grabbed a set of keys from the hooks by the door.

"Come on." He pulled at my hand. "Someone upset you. I'll drive your getaway car. Let's break free from here."

"Why?"

He shrugged.

"No. You're not coming along. I won't let you get into trouble for me."

Joe snorted. "As if it would be the first time. Anyway, I'm driving whether you want it or not. You're in no state of mind to sit behind a wheel right now. Please…let me." He picked up my suitcase and dropped it on the backseat of a black SUV.

"Nice ride."

He winked, and it dissolved some of the tension around us. "Jump in, girl."

After hesitating for a long minute, I hauled myself onto the passenger seat, blowing out all the air lodged in my lungs.

"Where are we heading?" the boy beside me asked, a crooked smile shaping his lips.

"No idea. Just keep driving. I wanna leave today behind."

"Then let's get lost."

The engine roared to life, and I relaxed in my seat, feeling free for the very first time in my entire existence.

Chapter 7

Joe

Grace snored softly next to me. We'd been on the road for a little over four hours, and she lost the fight two hours in, her body surrendering to sleep after all the tears she cried. My dad had been blowing up my phone for almost the entire time. At one point, I texted him back that I wasn't in the mood to talk and Grace was fine and we'd chat later. I said I was sorry for bailing on them and that something came up and I had to take care of it.

My gaze lingered on Grace's profile, lit only by the streetlights lining the interstate. Still wearing my suit jacket over what remained of her gown, she seemed at peace. And as beautiful as the first time I laid eyes on her. And more forbidden than the second time we crossed paths. Now linked by the ties of matrimony.

My fingers itched to push the loose strands of her hair back.

To trace the length of her lips.

To hug her until the pain that had etched her features earlier vanished forever.

Five weeks ago, I had fallen under the charm of my stepsister. *Younger* stepsister. Nobody could ever extract that piece of information from me. Even under the threat of torture. This was one of those secrets better left buried. It didn't matter that Pennsylvania's age of consent laws didn't apply to us; being together still felt wrong in every way that mattered.

She stirred in her sleep, and soon her eyelids fluttered open.

"Hey. You hungry?"

She bobbed her head, looking like a little girl with her big doe eyes and pouty lips.

I turned in my seat to grab the bag of food from the backseat and handed it to her. "Here. It's not fancy, but it should do the job."

She dug into the paper bag for the two burgers I'd picked up from a takeout ten minutes earlier.

"You ate anything?" she asked, her voice strained from all the tears she had cried.

"Just had a snack. I was waiting for you to wake up."

Grace unwrapped a burger and placed it in my hand before doing the same with the second one. "Thanks. For the food." She devoured hers in no time as if she'd been starving for months. In a sense, I bet she was.

"Will you tell me what your mother said that made you want to run away?"

She shrugged, the sleep not yet erased from her features. "She got mad about the dress. Spilled a load of bullshit on me. Said I was trying to steal her thunder and that she was ashamed of me. The…huh…usual. The accusations just weighed too heavy this time, you know? Like nothing I do is ever good enough. This gown," she pointed to herself, "looks amazing. I know I did a great job. Yet she had to insult me and say I ruined the dress she'd bought two sizes too small on purpose."

"It's on her. She made you feel bad about yourself. She's the one who should be ashamed of herself."

She nibbled on a piece of fry. "I'm used to it… My armor cracked this time. I'm done feeling unimportant. I'm going after my freedom. I wanna be happy, and I don't recall the last time I truly was or when I laughed my heart out." She cast a quick glance in my direction. "Except for the one night in a dive bar…but hey, even that doesn't count anymore."

"Well, when you were sleeping, I called Andy, you know my friend who played at the wedding. I had to explain why I ditched him without a warning. He told me your mother got into a crying fit when she realized we were gone. My dad comforted her and convinced her to give us some slack and to enjoy their night. Then I talked to my father. He knows we're together and we're both safe and sound." I paused. "And there's something else. The theatre I played at on Broadway has been flooded. The show is on a hiatus and should only resume in January. I learned it last night but didn't say anything because I wasn't sure if I wanted to stay in Silverville or not. I need a vacation. To clear my head and just let go for a while. Whatever you wanna do, I'm all yours. Until further notice."

"I'm sorry…about your job."

"Don't be. I'm exhausted. The break will do me good, I swear."

"Oh…okay. You didn't have to come along, but thank you for sticking with me. I feel better knowing we're in this together. I promise we'll make your time worth it."

"What about school?" I asked.

"I can do remote learning. If you justify my absence, they won't mind. After all, we're related now, and you're over twenty-one."

"I'll deal with it. Only if you promise you won't get behind."

"I'll do my best, Joe. Just don't take me back there. I can't deal with my mother; she overstepped this time and said horrible things…"

I squeezed her hand. "I won't. So, here are our options. We drive until we reach Florida. It may take a few days. We could go to California, but it's a bit of a stretch. My cousin Mason, who was at the wedding, lives in North Carolina. We could also go there. I heard there is a winter festival in Georgia but not sure when it starts exactly. We could look it up in the morning."

"Okay."

"I could offer to get shit-faced, but we're both aware it didn't end well for us in the past."

"No drinking. I'm not in the mood anyway." She pulled her sleeves over her hands.

"You cold?"

"A little. Do you maybe wanna stop for the night? I could use a hot shower and a bed."

I stared at Grace, not sure if she was serious because the last time we went to a hotel together…well… My body overheated at the memory.

"Joe. Stop. I'm sure we can share a room without jumping each other's bones," she added as if she was reading my thoughts. "We're siblings now, so it's different." She watched me, waiting for me to agree. Or not.

"All right. It's a plan." I took the next exit as billboards advertising lodging and restaurants polluted the side of the road.

Lying on the mattress I called dibs on, I waited for

Grace to finish showering in the adjacent small bathroom. The room we'd booked was kinda small. Two double beds, a wooden dresser, a tiny, under-the-counter refrigerator, and an en-suite bathroom. Pale-green wallpaper covered the walls, matching the comforters on the beds. We were in the middle of nowhere. Seriously, I had no idea what state or town we were in, but I didn't really care. All I cared about was getting Grace as far away from her mother as possible. For her own sanity.

I tried to focus my attention on the movie playing on the TV set on the dresser in front of me. Knowing Grace was naked on the other side of the door turned out to be a huge distraction. One I didn't need.

She stepped into the room, wearing only a loose T-shirt that I recognized as the one I lent her the night we spent together over a month ago.

An adorable blush covered her cheeks. "I'm sorry. I packed random stuff, and this is the only decent thing I have to sleep in."

I blinked. After wearing my jacket, she was now wearing my T-shirt. The thought she kept it pleased me more than it should.

That night really meant something to her too.

I jumped to my feet, needing to put some much-required distance between us. "All fine. I'll shower now. We'll have to go shopping tomorrow because we left in a hurry, and I brought nothing along with me."

"Sure."

Thirty minutes later, after I turned the nightlight off, wearing only my boxer briefs, I slid under the covers.

"You asleep?" I asked my bed neighbor.

"Nah. My brain won't shut up."

We remained silent for a while.

"Joe, if I came to sleep next to you, would it be all right

or just weird? I'm kinda sad in my heart, and I could really use a hug."

I debated the idea in my mind. I knew what playing with fire looked like, and still, I couldn't find in me the strength to deny her. I flipped the covers over. "Come here. I'll provide the arms."

The whiff of her shampoo hit my nostrils first, followed by the sweet scent of her. I kept my hand firmly attached to her shoulder, locking all my filthy thoughts in a place where I couldn't easily access them.

The feel of Grace in my arms eased every cell in me. My heart rate decreased. My muscles relaxed. And my mind went blank.

Nestled against her, listening to her soft breaths, I drifted into a deep slumber.

"What's that?" Grace asked from beside me. She perused the area around us with big, wondrous eyes. We took an exit toward Mistletoe Creek, Tennessee when the fuel gauge indicated we were almost out of gas. Mistletoe Creek was on the Tennessee side of the Smoky Mountains. A six-hour drive toward our destination.

This morning we weighed our options and decided to head toward Feather Lake, North Carolina, where my cousin Mason and his wife Melinda lived. I had called him earlier, and after I explained the situation to him, he had offered us the apartment over the garage he owned until Grace and I could figure out our next move.

Looking for a gas station, we passed a group of people dressed like elves and a Santa with a bell in hand standing by the front door of a little shop and asking for donations for people in need.

Pine wreaths hung from the street light poles, and giant candy canes lined the sidewalks. Wood deer made of logs and branches stood on each corner of the intersection. Handcrafted snowmen had been propped in front of each business.

"Mistletoe Creek looks like a Christmas town," Grace exclaimed. "You know, like in the movies." We parked in front of Gold's Gas & Garage. "It's beautiful. Ohmygod, it really looks like it has come straight from an old movie set." White siding and a red roof, it had open garage doors for mechanical purposes and old gas pumps with a nineteen-sixties vibe.

Grace was right. This town had undeniable appeal, showcasing the magic of the Holidays, not a care in the world we were still almost a month away from Christmas.

I stopped the engine and opened the door. "Gimme a sec. I'll be right back."

"Take your time," Grace said. "I'm in no hurry to leave this place."

The fresh scent of pine filled the air, and I took a full whiff in, enjoying how it tickled my nose.

I was about to fill the car when a woman walked by. "Are you new in town?" she asked, stopping beside me.

"Just passing through," I said. "It's lovely here. Love the holiday vibe you've got going on around town."

"Too bad you're not here to stay. Our calendar is packed with celebrations all the way through the New Year. If you're not in a rush, there is the tree lighting celebration in the main square tonight. You should come. The whole town will be there. There will be music and hot chocolate."

"I'll ask my…huh…Grace. We could maybe stay overnight. If we can find a hotel or something." I had no idea how to explain the relationship between Grace and me to a stranger. Calling her a sister felt weird, and a friend seemed too impersonal. From now on, I would stick to her name.

The woman grinned. "It's your lucky day. I run the Stardust Inn. We have one room left for tonight." She extended her arm. "I'm Lea. Lea Delaney."

I slipped my palm into hers. "Joe. Crawford."

"It's nice to meet you, Joe. The inn is about half a mile down this way," she said, pointing to our left. "You'll pass the Glass Slipper Bed & Breakfast, The Woodsman—the tavern—and it'll be right after. You won't miss it."

"Thanks."

"See you later. Maybe."

"Yeah, maybe," I called after her.

"Okay, hear me out," I told Grace when I climbed back behind the steering wheel. I rubbed my hands together, warming them up. With the cold front settling all over eastern Tennessee, I wondered if we'd get snow within a few days. "I saw the sparkles in your eyes earlier, and we're in no rush. How about we stay here for a night? There's a Christmas tree lighting celebration later. Could be fun to join the festivities. What do you think?"

She tapped her chin with a finger, twisting her lips. "Yeah. Okay. I love the idea."

"Perfect. I found us a place to crash overnight."

Her eyes rounded. "You did? Already?"

"Yep. Let's enjoy ourselves tonight, and tomorrow we'll get back on the road."

"Joe, thanks for doing this with me. Not a lot of people have made me feel special over the years. I appreciate your trying."

She fidgeted with her hands, and I had to firm my grip around the steering wheel to avoid taking her hand in mine. "I'm sorry you ever thought you were not good enough."

Grace cast a glance down. "It's hard living in her shadow, you know. My mom was a beauty pageant queen. She modeled for magazines and walked the runway for the best designers in Milan and Paris. I just wish she would accept me the way I am and not ask me to be someone else —someone I'm not—all the time. It gets exhausting in the end."

"I can't pretend I can relate to that because my dad has always been awesome. Even when he was heartbroken after my mom's death, he was still trying. I was the one who acted out for a while. He never lost faith in me. Whenever you wanna talk, I'm here."

"Thanks."

"Let's make a deal, though. Let's forget about your mom for the time being. The best way not to let her invade your thoughts is not to give her power over them."

"You think I can do that?"

I nodded. "Sure. Take back control of your thoughts. Every time you hear her insult you in your head, switch what she says for a positive affirmation." I paused, gathering my thoughts. "If her voice in your head tells you that you should…let's say…change clothes because it doesn't suit your figure, then rephrase it to *I look beautiful, no matter how I dress.*"

"You believe it'll work?"

"Yeah. I had a teacher in college who would train us to reword our drowning thoughts before a performance. To kill the little voice in our head telling us we weren't good enough."

"Oh. I can try."

"I know you can, Grace. You can do anything you put your mind to. Never let anyone tell you otherwise."

We remained silent for a full minute.

"Ohmygod, is this—?" Grace's attention drifted

between me and the building in front of us. Baby yellow siding, white trims, round windows, the place seemed to be out of a cartoon. An igloo made of fake ice was set in the front yard. "Stardust Inn. We're staying *here*?"

"Well, that's the plan. You want to?"

Happiness illuminated her face. "Are you kidding me? I love it."

"Then let's go inside."

Chapter 8
Grace

"This is your room," Lea announced, pride lacing her voice, as she opened the door. I scanned the small space. Maple wooden floors, off-white walls, a large round window framed with velvet steel blue curtains, an upholstered chair in the same shade of blue, a dresser, and two matching nightstands. Stardust Inn was adorable and pleased me a lot. Until I noticed the bed. As in *one* bed. "The guests who booked the room are delayed and will only arrive tomorrow, so it's yours for the night if you desire."

"Is the entire inn fully booked?" I asked, trying not to sound ungrateful.

"Yes. This time of the year is our busiest. People make reservations months in advance. They come from all over the country. Some even fly from Europe to spend a month here. You're lucky I have an opening at the last minute."

I forced my lips into an upside curl. "We'll take it."

Lea clasped her hands before her, her smile unwavering. "Awesome. Get settled and meet me downstairs when you're ready."

"Deal."

With a sigh, I dropped on the white-linen comforter the moment the door clicked shut after her. It felt as if I was lying on a cloud. *One bed.* After we fell asleep in each other's arms last night, Joe and I promised it would never happen again. No need to tempt ourselves. Our attraction and chemistry hadn't diminished over time. Even after our parents got married, the sparks between us were still present every time we were in each other's presence. Lust wasn't a faucet you could turn off. No matter how much you longed to.

The door opened, and I sprang to a sitting position on the bed.

"Grace, I'm back," Joe said, his smile slipping when he noticed the queen-size bed taking most of the room. He had gone shopping for a few necessities and clothes after dropping me here. "Oh."

"Yep." I popped the *P*. "I'm sure can work something out. After all, it's just for a night."

He lowered the bags he was holding onto the dresser and came to sit beside me. "I can sleep on the floor. It's no big deal. I'm sure there are extra covers and pillows somewhere I can use."

"I can sleep in the chair. I'm shorter than you. I'll make it work."

"I would never let you. Told you once I wasn't a jerk."

"But I insist."

"You're stubborn, girl. Let's fight about it later. Wanna grab some food? I'm starving. I spotted a coffee shop down the road. We could walk there. I got you a sweater just in case you didn't bring enough warm clothes."

"You did?"

He nodded, fishing the clothes and toiletries out of the bags he discarded earlier. "Here."

I burst into laughter. "You got me a Mistletoe Creek sweater? How thoughtful of you. I'll have a souvenir forever." My laughter died down. "Thank you. Seriously, I appreciate it."

"The fun thing is that I bought a matching one for myself. Along with a pair of jeans, a few shirts, and sneakers. I love the wedding attire I'm wearing, but I can't wait to change out of it." Joe was still dressed in his suit, minus the tie he had ditched ten minutes into our road trip. I wouldn't complain because he looked very hot and masculine dressed like this with the shirt sleeves rolled up to his elbows and exposing his corded forearms. Every time I glanced at him, I could feel my body temperature soaring.

Stop looking at him like he's a potential lover, Grace, I chastised myself.

"Gimme a few minutes to shower and change, and I'll be all yours," he said. He didn't make any move to enter the bathroom. Instead, his gaze stole mine.

Our eyes fixated on each other for the longest time. His Adam's apple bobbed, and I followed the movement of his throat.

All mine. If only it were true.

Why did just a look from him still make me weak in the knees?

Clearly, my body hadn't gotten the memo where it concerned him and our complicated relationship.

He pointed behind him, breaking the moment. "I-I'll just go now."

Joe's expression turned boyish like he'd been caught doing something he shouldn't, and I failed at not smiling.

"Yeah, go. I think I can manage for ten more minutes by myself."

He added nothing, and seconds later, the door clicked behind him.

The suffocating tension in the air finally evaporated.

Fluffing my hair with my fingers, I checked my reflection in the full-length mirror hung behind the door and slipped the Mistletoe Creek sweater over my head, loving how it looked paired with the jeans I was wearing. Navy with a varsity-style design, it was a bit loose, but I loved the feel of it. It reminded me of the times I'd worn Joe's clothes before. Each time I did, it made me feel special. That morning after we spent the night together, I didn't mean to steal his T-shirt. But I also couldn't find it in me to give it back. It was the only tangible memory of the night we shared. The only thing reminding me it really did happen and I hadn't dreamed it.

For a second, as I stared at the girl in the mirror, I imagined what it would be like to wear his clothes more often. I couldn't tell if it was the clean and manly scent of him clinging to the fibers that brought me comfort or just the fact they were his.

Tying my hair in a sleek ponytail, I admired myself one last time. Satisfied, I spent some time contemplating the town through the window. It was the cutest place I had ever come across. People with huge smiles filled the sidewalks.

A mother pushed two young children in a stroller using her elbows, manning a black Labrador puppy's leash with one hand and a coffee cup in the other. The sight of them made me smile.

A guy and a girl about my age walked side by side, the guy stealing glances at the girl, the latter oblivious to the love simmering in his eyes as she talked, gesturing with her hands.

A little girl with pigtails and owl-patterned earmuffs walked with a white Persian cat in a backpack, and a man, whom I assumed to be her father, held her hand while talking on the phone.

In the distance, I could see a building that resembled a castle, and I wondered what it was.

"Ready?" Joe asked from behind me, putting an end to my people-watching moment.

"Yeah. Sure."

I turned around and smiled, trying to appear unaffected as my eyes trailed the length of him. In dark jeans that hung low on his hips and a fit, long-sleeved black V-neck shirt that molded to his chest, Joe was too hot for his own good. Couldn't he look ugly for once? Just so my body wouldn't react to his and I would stop ogling him.

I cleared my throat and spun around to grab my purse. "Let's go."

Keeping a safe distance between us, we ambled down the sidewalk I had admired just minutes ago, heading toward the coffee shop Joe had told me about. Christmas music played from speakers mounted on the streetlights. A faint scent of cinnamon and pine lingered in the air.

"It even smells like Christmas here," Joe said. "Walking around makes my mouth water."

I chuckled. "Yeah. I bet people here are always hungry. Restaurants must be a popular industry."

"I hope the food here tastes as good as it smells." He linked our hands, tugging me forward. "Come on, I'm starving."

Everyone we crossed paths with either nodded at us or greeted us with a warm "How's it going?"

"Can you believe how nice people are here?" Joe asked.

"I think it's the whole holiday thing they've got going on. It's festive, and it makes people happy."

He released me and stuffed his hands in his pockets. A tiny piece of me hated the idea that I'd prefer if he still held my hand in his instead. I debated inching closer to him and pressing my side against his, but I shook my head, pushing the temptation away before I did something awkward.

I had no reason to want to feel his warmth or his skin against mine. I was just being stupid.

Why couldn't my body understand once and for all? Joe and I were not meant to be. The attraction had to die and be buried before it consumed me.

The coffee shop was as cute as the rest of the town. The outside consisted of white brick walls and teal awnings. The inside looked a bit more rustic. Worn wooden floors, exposed brick walls, black wrought iron chandeliers, powder-blue chairs spread around square maple tables. A large painting of a scene I recognized as Main Street covered the wall behind the counter where a selection of croissants, bagels, and scones were spread. Three high-end coffee makers were set on the left, and a barista dressed as a gingerbread man was busy filling orders.

Christmas music played on the speakers embedded in the ceiling.

A couple in their fifties, sporting matching ugly Christmas sweaters, were sipping hot chocolate, nibbling on snowflake-shaped sugar cookies, and gazing at each other with love.

A family of six sat by the window, enjoying croissants while playing a game of *I spy with my little eye*, Christmas edition. They were all smiling, even the baby in the high-chair clapping his hands, drool covering his chin.

Three women about my grandmother's age were knitting something resembling scarves, laughing at what one of them said.

Joe and I sat in the back corner. He opened the town schedule on his phone. "Okay, they're really going all in on the holiday theme," he said. *"Gingerbread Decorating Contest, Masquerade Ball, Breakfast with Santa, Carolers in the Town Square.* They know how to keep themselves and the town busy."

"Lea told me people come from far away to attend the festivities."

"It's impressive." He pointed to something on the screen. "They even have a Christmas light fight, whatever it is."

I propped my elbows up on the table and rested my chin on my joined hands. "I wish I could live here full time. I don't know. It must be something in the air, or it's due to their holiday spirit, but the residents of Mistletoe Creek seem laid-back." I sighed. "I would kill for an existence void of stress and the need to please everyone."

Joe bit into his raspberry scone and moaned. "Fuck, this is good."

I chuckled. He looked like a little boy right now, a mischievous glow lighting up his face, thanks to his chin dimple.

He brought the pastry to my lips. "Taste it." My first reflex was to refuse. After all, I'd been conditioned all my life to avoid sugar, carbs, and empty calories. Joe must have read the uncertainty on my face because he added, "Grace, you're beautiful the way you are. Don't let anyone tell you otherwise. Take a bite. You only have one life to live. Don't miss out on something because it scares you."

"I'm not scared."

"Your mom is sick between her ears. I'm not saying to

eat a dozen scones in one go, but you're allowed to enjoy the fun stuff."

Growing up, I had always cheated on the diet my mother imposed on me. It counted as a small act of rebellion. Now that she wasn't here, I felt bad about eating stuff she wouldn't approve of. My brain had gotten all mixed up. The circuits had overheated. Sometimes, even I had a hard time following its reasoning.

I tried Joe's trick. Instead of *I'm not allowed to eat sweets*, I rephrased it as *I'm allowed to enjoy fun food from time to time*.

I exhaled. "Fine. One bite." I parted my lips, and Joe positioned the scone between them as I bit into the pastry. "Ohmygod, it's more than good. Wow, it's amazing." I licked my lips, not wanting to waste any of the delicious filling.

Joe pushed his plate in front of me. "Here, take it. I'll get another one."

"You sure?"

"Affirmative." He stood up and went to wait in line at the counter.

The place buzzed with people this morning, and I wondered if it was always busy.

"Okay," Joe said as he sat back next to me. "Hear me out. I think we should stay here… For a little while at least. You said so yourself—you wish you could live here full-time. The lady behind the counter knows someone who knows someone else who is renting gingerbread house cabins in the mountains. It would be perfect for us. She messaged somebody, and they said we could move in tonight and stay until early January. Since we arrived here, timing has been on our side. We should make the most of it. The cabin is a bit old, but she assured me it's clean and safe. It comes with everything, except food and our personal belongings. What do you say?"

Never before had I noticed Joe being super enthusiastic about something, and I was glad he was lowering his walls around me. Maybe he really did need this vacation after all.

"Okay, let's do this. Let's stay here for a month and see if it's as perfect as it appears to be or if it's all fake. Perhaps their happiness will rub off on us."

We shook on it. "Deal."

Chapter 9

Joe

With Grace nestled between my arms and her back pressed against my front, we watched the tree lighting ceremony. The energy was electric tonight. Lea didn't lie. The whole town had gathered in the town center, waiting for the mayor to turn the lights on.

The town square was a patch of lawn delimited by Main Street, surrounded by a dozen local businesses. Tonight, people sat on lawn chairs, wrapped in blankets, sipping hot drinks from thermoses as they waited for the tree lighting ceremony to begin. Just like the movies, it was the perfect small-town set-up. Even I could envision snow falling on Christmas morning as families, buried under warm jackets and fluffy hats, gathered here to build snowmen.

In a white gazebo in the middle of the square, a group of carolers dressed in red jackets and matching hats sang

Christmas songs in front of a small crowd who sang along. Golden Christmas lights had been wrapped around the edges of the structure, giving the gazebo a fairy-tale appearance.

Peppermint and fresh pine aromas lingered in the crisp night air.

The cold stung my ears, and I lowered the knitted hat I bought earlier from a small shop across the street to keep snug.

I had never meant for Grace and me to be bundled up together, but when she began shivering fifteen minutes ago, and neither of us was wearing clothes warm enough to fight the cold, I pulled her against me, hoping it would do the trick to warm us up.

Each time she swayed her hips to the rhythm of the music, I grew tighter in my pants. I couldn't tell if she could sense that the simple movement affected me through the multiple layers of clothes separating our bodies, but if she did, she said nothing about it.

She turned in my arms and lifted the to-go cup of caffeine we'd been sharing to my mouth, and I took a sip, careful not to burn my tongue.

Our gazes collided, and it felt as if I'd been punched in the chest. My breath caught in my lungs. She had no idea how gorgeous she was. With her white faux fur earmuffs and big eyes, she watched me like I knew secrets she couldn't wait for me to share. She smiled, and an earthquake exploded in my chest. Every moment in her company made it harder for me to hide my attraction toward her. When I looked at Grace, I didn't just wanna rip her clothes off and fuck her. I wanted to cherish her, to care for her, to love her. It was fifty shades of bad ideas, and still, I couldn't care less. The only thing preventing me from kissing her the way she deserved was her age and the fact we were kind-of related. No way would I jeopardize our already complicated relationship and fragile new family bond just because I couldn't keep it in my pants. That was where I drew the line.

When I checked last night, in a moment of weakness, because I couldn't abandon myself to sleep, I had learned that according to Pennsylvania laws, our relationship wouldn't be frowned upon. In Tennessee, though, Grace had to be eighteen to consent to a relationship with someone older. I would never put us at risk. No matter how strong the temptation was.

All the people on the quad started counting, freeing me from my thoughts.

"*Ten... Nine... Eight... Seven... Six... Five...*"

Grace and I joined in, the excitement of the moment permeating the air.

She clasped her hands under her chin and turned around, ready for the tree to illuminate the night.

"*Four... Three... Two... One...*"

Hundreds of lights twinkled before our eyes.

The huge fir turned into a giant constellation right before us.

Some people applauded, while others admired the sparkling masterpiece with stars in their eyes.

"It's beautiful," Grace said, tipping her head back until she could look at me. "I feel like a little girl right now. I'm glad we decided to stay."

"Me too."

"Thanks for bringing the magic back into my life, Joe. You have no idea how precious it is to me. I never truly enjoyed the holidays growing up. I'm glad I finally have the chance to."

I leaned forward, my lips a hair's breadth away from her ear. "Grace, magic is back in my life too. All because of you. I didn't realize how robotic and predictable my existence had become before I met you. You bring a wave of freshness into my days. I'm thankful."

She was about to say something when Lea neared us, putting to rest our heartfelt moment. "Hey, guys. I'm so happy you stayed tonight. How do you like the town so far?"

Grace smiled, and the sight weakened my knees. The apples of her cheeks were reddened, thanks to the cold night air, and her irises reflected the lights of the giant tree. She really seemed happy. And carefree.

"We love it. Like a lot. It's so festive, and everyone has been super nice and welcoming so far. This is magical. I understand why people come here at this time of the year." She glanced at me. "We love the town so much that we've decided to stay for a little while longer."

"You have? Amazing. What a great news." A woman joined us. "Oh, and this is Rose. She's the marketing person for the Southern Brothers Brewing." She gestured to Grace and me. "This is the couple who stayed at the inn last night. Joe and Grace."

"Are you enjoying yourselves?" Rose asked.

"We are," I replied.

"Mistletoe Creek will grow on you. Take my word for it. You'll see it when you leave. A slice of your heart will forever remain here."

Lea nodded in agreement. "We'll let you two lovebirds be."

"We're not... It's not..." *Nice job, man.* I couldn't even define Grace's and my relationship.

"There's someone I must talk to. I'll see you two later," Lea said before traipsing away.

"Enjoy your night," Rose added before I could clarify the fact Grace and I were not a couple. "I hope to see more of you sometime soon." She waved at us as she went to meet a group of people further on our left.

Once both women were far enough, Grace stared at me. "Joe, how are we supposed to explain our complex relationship to people? *Friends* feels wrong, and *siblings* has a weird ring to it."

I shrugged. "No idea." If only she knew how hard I'd been trying to explain it to myself for weeks now and failing every time.

Silence fell upon us.

Two little boys wearing matching royal-blue jackets and red hats neared us. They looked so much alike that no doubt they were brothers.

"Who are you?" the older one, who looked to be around six, asked.

"I'm Joe. And this is Grace."

"Are you new in town?" the younger boy asked.

"We're just visiting. For a few weeks," I said.

"Oh," both boys exclaimed. "We live here. On Reindeer Way. In a red house."

"Thomas. Mama said we're not allowed to give personal information to strangers," the older boy said, shaking his head.

"They're not strangers. Their names are Joe and Grace." The younger boy smiled, showing a missing tooth.

"That's not how it works. Come on, we should go." The older brother grabbed the younger one's hand, but the small boy refused to follow him.

"I don't want to go now." He turned to face Grace. "You are pretty. Super pretty. Like a princess. Isn't she pretty, Julian?"

His brother nodded. "Yes."

"Well, thank you," Grace said, the color on her cheeks darkening. "I would love to be a real princess."

"You are. This is a magic town. And pretty girls are always princesses in magic towns," the older boy said. "Mama says so. Have you been to the castle yet?"

"A castle? I saw it earlier and wondered what it was."

"It's a real castle. You should go and see it," the older boy said.

"Thanks for the information. We'll look it up," I said.

A woman, bundled up in a bright-pink parka, waved at the boys.

"Oh, we should go," Thomas said. "Bye."

They ran toward who I assumed was their mother.

"Well, that was interesting," Grace said. "Weren't they adorable? And they said I look like a princess. How sweet."

"They didn't lie, you know. You really look like one."

She averted her gaze, staring in the distance and rocking back and forth on her heels. I used one finger to turn her face so I could level our eyes. "It's true. It's about time you accept compliments. You are beautiful, Grace."

"Huh, thanks."

"You are. Never doubt it."

Without a warning, she wrapped her arms around me. I stiffened, before relaxing against her. "Thanks, Joe."

I planted a kiss on the top of her head but said nothing as a cocktail of feelings rose inside me and messed with all my resolve.

"Wanna go and see that cabin now?" I asked when Grace stepped back. "The lady I talked to on the phone said there was a fireplace. We could light it up and make the place ours. What do you think?"

"I'd like that. I was thinking of calling it a night anyway."

Walking to our car following a back alley, we arrived in front of a small village exhibition made of five-foot-tall buildings. A bakery, a school, a hospital, a dozen houses, and half-sized characters. Fake trees and snow completed the magical display.

"It's so cool. I'm speechless," Grace announced.

"Me too." I grabbed her hand as we admired every glittering piece. "It really is impressive." Next to me, Grace shivered, and I tugged at her hand. "Let's get out of here."

A minute later, we reached the car and cranked up the heat as we drove through town, heading toward the mountains. Twice, we had to stop to admire the decor. Enveloped in hundreds of light garlands, entire streets brightened the dark night. Inflatable snowmen, Santas, and reindeers filled the front yards.

In every park or green space we passed, there were trios of lit Christmas trees on display.

"It feels like we're living in a dream," I said. "I don't have enough eyes to take it all in."

"We should come here every year. Make it a tradition. It's impossible to be sad when you live in Mistletoe Creek. From now on, it will forever be my happy place."

Grace read the directions on my phone that the woman I rented the place from had sent me .Navigating the steep, dark roads at this late hour turned out to be more challenging than I would have thought.

"I think it's the third one on our left," Grace said as she repeated the directions for the second time. "We should arrive in three…two…one…" I stopped in front of a long driveway. It was so dark we couldn't see anything. "Joe, are you sure we're not lost? It's kind of scary out here."

I looked around us. Grace was right. We could barely see five feet ahead of us. I had no idea if other people lived around. I scratched my head after I checked the map once more. "It's supposed to be here." I released the brake and pressed on the gas, turning into the driveway. Moonbeams filtered through the tall trees surrounding the property. It seemed like we were entering a haunted forest.

The cabin appeared in front of us at the end of the driveway.

From here, it didn't look like anything the lady had promised. Somber and uninviting, I was tempted to drive around and leave. Curiosity got the better of me, so I put the car in park but left the engine running. Just in case. "Gimme a sec. I'll see if I can find a light switch. I'm sure we can illuminate this place."

"You're going to leave me alone?" Grace's voice quivered as her eyes darted between me and the house. "Are you sure it's safe to go in?"

"There's only one way to find out."

"Oh. Be careful then."

I exited the comfort of the car, my body on high alert and my hands balled into fists at my sides. Standing on the threshold, I punched in the four-digit code the woman had sent me on the touchpad lock before stepping inside. My chest constricted. I couldn't see a thing and had to sidestep to the right so that the car's headlights cast a glow inside. Why did I leave my phone in the car?

A chill ran through me. This place required warmth. And lights. I ran my hand over the wall on my left, and my fingers connected with a light switch. The exterior of the cabin turned into a light show when I flicked it on. "Whoa." I blinked, dazzled by the colorful display as I returned outside. We hadn't just rented a cabin in the woods; we really had booked an oversized gingerbread house.

Grace exited the car and came to stand next to me. "Joe…it's…wow."

"I know."

She slipped her mittened hand inside mine as we stood still, soaking up every detail.

The exterior siding was dark brown wood. Multicolor masses resembling candies lined all the edges, and what looked like giant lollipops framed each side of the front door. Fake dripping snow resembling icing covered the roof under a layer of dozens of oversized red and white starlight mints. Candy canes acted as shutters on both sides of every window.

I blinked, at a loss for words.

I felt like a kid in a sweet shop, unable to stop salivating at the display.

Grace tugged me forward. "Let's see the inside."

The first floor consisted of a small kitchen doubling as a dining room and a living room. A large double-face boulder fireplace stood in the middle. The lingering scent of burning wood filled the air and regaled my nose. Like the exterior, there were touches of color everywhere inside too, but mostly in the form of accessories. Candy-shaped pillows. Lime-green throws. Multicolored kitchen chairs. Paintings of desserts on the walls. A fully decorated Christmas tree occupied the far corner, and the delicious fragrance of the freshly cut pine filled the house. Light garlands had been wrapped around the banister leading to the second floor.

Upstairs were three bedrooms. A larger one and two smaller ones. The small ones shared a Jack and Jill bathroom while the master one had its own en-suite. Each bedroom had been designed according to a theme. White and silver winter wonderland. Red and black lumberjack plaid decor. And navy blue and gold midnight hour.

"Ohmygoodness, this is beautiful," Grace exclaimed from beside me, grinning like I had just offered her the world. She jumped into my embrace before I had time to react, locking her arms around my neck. "Thank you for this."

My arms wrapped around her body of their own volition for the second time in less than an hour. This time, I held her against my pounding heart. Fuck, why did it always feel like our bodies were made to fit perfectly when molded together?

No matter how much I tried to stay indifferent to her charisma, I kept failing.

Grace's happiness overload faded as we stared at each other. Reality hit us like a cold shower.

"We shouldn't…" I muttered.

"I-I'm sorry…for my…huh…enthusiasm. I'll try to dial it down a notch from now on."

I cleared my throat and erased all the thoughts of her lips on mine swimming in my mind. "Don't be. I'm glad you're happy."

"I am." She stepped back. "I won't attack you like this again. It was…huh…inappropriate?"

It sounded more like a question than a comment.

It's not inappropriate, I wanted to argue. *Please keep doing it.*

Instead, I kept my mouth shut.

"I'll get our stuff from the car." I turned to leave, sucking a full breath in to release every particle of tension clinging to me.

I lit up the fireplace, and since we had stopped by the grocery store on our way here to grab some necessities, I busied myself emptying the bags, while Grace offered to set up the bedrooms and unpack our luggage. She assigned me the lumberjack-themed room after I insisted she take the master midnight-hour bedroom.

On my phone, I played some music, humming and keeping my brain occupied so it couldn't nag me about why I chose to spend a month in a cabin with a girl who got me all tangled up inside. I had no recollection of the last time I'd been so confused in my life.

A scratching sound coming from the front door captured my attention and released me from my drowning thoughts.

Could it be a bear?

After all, we were in the middle of the woods in the mountains. Bears, elks, bobcats. Any creature could be standing on our front porch right now.

I hated the fact the door had no glass panel and that I had to open it to see who stood on the other side. The last thing I wished for was an intruder to walk in unannounced. One with claws and an appetite for human beings.

Armed with a kitchen knife, I yanked the door open and looked around. Nothing. All I could see were the blinding lights emanating from the cabin and the thick forest ahead.

I closed my eyes, focusing on the sounds around me. The breeze. An owl. And maybe a deer.

Something pushed against my shin. I opened my lids, and when I glanced down, my heart melted. A tiny gray kitten bunted my leg. I bent forward to pick him up. "Hey you. How did you get here? Are you lost? Want to come in?"

The small ball of fur purred in response.

"You must be freezing. Let's go inside. We'll warm you up."

I put down the knife on the coffee table, and using a pillow from the couch, I set the little one by the fireplace. After looking up what to feed him online, I whipped up a homemade milk replacer with ingredients we'd just picked up.

He lapped up some of the milk—he was a male, I'd checked—and fell asleep within a minute.

I watched him for a moment, unable to take my eyes off his tiny figure.

Climbing the stairs, I felt a buzz of excitement at the thought of Grace meeting our new roommate. I heard her before I saw her. She was in her bedroom, emptying her bag and swaying to a melody she was humming. Kill. Me. Now.

I wasn't allowed to find her pretty. Or even sexy.

Those thoughts had to dissipate, or they would ruin me.

She had changed into a pair of fussy leggings and a long sweater. Her hair was piled on the top of her head, loose strands framing her face. Since we had run away from our parents' wedding, she hadn't applied makeup once. The thought she didn't need her armor around me pleased me. A little too much.

With a roll of my shoulders, I tried to erase the tension crippling me and knocked on the ajar door. "Hey. I have a surprise for you downstairs when you're ready."

Grace turned around, her face flushing as if I'd caught her doing something naughty. If only…

"Surprise? Care to explain? Is it hot chocolate? Because I could use a hot beverage right now before going to bed."

"I can make you a mug later, but it's something else. Much more exciting."

Her lips twisted. "Will I be in trouble?"

I grinned, shaking my head. "Not this time."

"You sure?"

I smirked. "Why? You wanna be in trouble?"

"Mayb—" She pinched her lips together and shook her head a few times. "Nope. Not this time." She eyed me, not shying away from the attraction simmering between us. Her pupils darkened. Her lips parted on an exhale.

Even though we both promised we'd do our best to kill the attraction we experienced every time we stood too close to each other, we were failing. We stood still, the air around us crackling with electricity. One month together in closed proximity would no doubt be the worst kind of torture. I wondered how long we could resist the pull before we had to walk away.

Grace's chest moved with each intake of air. I forced my attention back to her face. I could read the same warning signs that I'd observed on the night we met, dancing in her dark irises. The girl loved trouble. And from the glints in her eyes, she appeared to love it even more when I was involved.

I scratched the back of my head and stared at my feet, breaking the eye contact. "About that surprise… Huh, are you coming?"

The spell we were under evaporated. "Yeah, sure. Show me."

She followed me down the stairs, and when we inched closer to the fireplace, I said, "Close your eyes."

"Why?"

"Because it will be more fun. Trust me."

She sighed. "Fine."

I pulled her forward and angled her body toward the little furry ball. "I'm telling you, your heart may not recover, and you may fall in love. I'll do my best to provide what it needs as long as you accept to co-parent with me."

She tensed beside me. "Joe, are you pregnant?"

"Ha. Ha. You think you're funny?" She shrugged. "Geez, woman. Open your eyes."

She glanced around until I pointed down at the floor.

"Ohmygod. How did you…?" Sparkles shone in her

eyes. "Joe, it's so tiny." She crouched, softly running her fingers over the head of our unexpected little guest.

"Grace, meet DH. DH, meet Grace."

She blinked, searching my gaze. "Wait… He already has a name? Was he wearing a collar or something?"

"Nope. I gave him one." I smiled big because I was so proud of my choice.

"You did?" A puzzling look painted her face. "DH? What does it mean? I would have chosen something like Mitten. Or Slipper. Maybe Rocky. Or Mozart. In your honor." That piece of information warmed my heart. "But not DH… Wanna be more specific?"

I shook my head. "Not sure I want to. Trust me, it's suiting. And it fits us both. Don't worry. He loves his name."

"And you know that how?"

"Because I'm his dad and he watched me with his little adorable eyes and nodded when I named him."

Grace grabbed a pillow and threw it at me. "You're ridiculous. Since you asked me to co-parent with you, can we discuss a real name?"

"Nope. Non-negotiable. DH is a real name, by the way. Like CJ or TJ."

"You're being a big baby about the whole thing."

"I stand by my choice."

"But what does it mean? Come on, Joe. Work with me here."

I pretended to zip my lips. "This will be the greatest mystery of your life. Unless you figure it out yourself."

She shook her head but couldn't hide her smile as she stared at the kitten. "Fine. DH it is. Can I hug him now?"

I nodded. "All yours to love."

She tucked the kitten into the crook of her arm, right

over her heart, and I swear my own heart melted a little. "We'll have to go shopping. Litter box, food, blanket."

"I fed him some milk replacer, cut up old newspapers I found to make a litter box until we can buy a real one, and noticed some blankets in the cupboard by the bathroom that we can use. He'll be fine for tonight."

"Oh, okay." Grace nuzzled DH's neck, and he purred. *I know the feeling, little man.* "Joe, can you believe we are parents now? It's a big commitment." Tenderness filled her gaze, and I wished it was aimed at me.

"Well, I wouldn't wanna do it with anyone else. Being a co-parent, I mean."

A fresh surge of tension rose between us, and I mentally chastised myself. I had to start keeping my thoughts to myself.

For everyone's sake.

Chapter 10

Joe

"Karaoke night is the best," Grace exclaimed as we sat around a small round table in front of the stage. We'd been in Mistletoe Creek for a week, and Grace had been talking about coming here for just as long.

"I never would have thought I'd ever go to a Christmas karaoke night. My friend Andy would have a good laugh. For years I teased him he should be a guitar-playing Santa and sing for old ladies in retirement homes during the holidays."

"Are you gonna get up there with me?" Glints of expectation shone in her eyes.

"Nope. I'm good just watching. I'll be the loudest clapper, though."

Her lips swelled into a pout. "You're no fun. Can you order me a drink while I go add my name to the list of performers?"

"Sure you really wanna do this?"

She nodded. "Yes." For a moment, she watched the couple onstage slurring the lyrics of what sounded like a Christmas song, but the drunken, unrecognizable version of it. "See? They're having the time of their lives." She left me alone, walking toward the stage with a pep in her step.

A waitress about my age, wearing a tiny red and white dress with long black hair and a rack impossible to miss, neared the table. "*Ho, ho, ho.*" She winked, pursing her red lips. "Welcome to Santa's Lodge. Are you new in town? I've never seen you around before."

"Just visiting."

"Alone?" she asked.

"No."

"Girlfriend?"

I sighed. What's with the twenty questions? She wouldn't get any intel from me. I knew this game all too well. "What's on the menu?"

A mischievous smirk shaped her lips. "Me. If you're naughty enough."

"I'm not these days, sorry. So, that menu…?"

She huffed, clearly annoyed that I wasn't playing along. I had no intention of befriending the server. Not tonight.

Her voice turned bored. "Today's special is our version of Eggnog and the Elf-Ale, our green draft beer."

"Green draft beer? Is it slimy?"

The girl laughed. "Nah." She paused. "I can work with a sense of humor."

I quirked one brow.

"Oh yeah, the Elf-Ale. Old plain beer with green food coloring. It's supposed to be more Christmassy."

"Oh. I'll stick to regular beer. Any Christmas-themed drinks with vodka?"

"Sure. The Silver Bell and The Midnight Star. The

first one is mixed with lime and the Midnight Star is more like a spiked lemonade."

"One Midnight Star, then."

"Good. I'll be right back." Her hand brushed my shoulder in a not-so-subtle attempt to let me know she was still interested. I knew her type. I'd fucked dozens of girls like her in the past.

She flashed me a large smile over her shoulder and sashayed toward the bar. I ignored her and brought my attention back to the couple rocking the stage, belting out the lyrics of a song I still couldn't recognize.

"I'm sixth on the list," Grace said as she joined me and sat back in her seat.

Santa's Lodge was small. No more than six people could sit at the bar. Fourteen small round tables were scattered around the space, battery-operated candles set in the middle of each one, giving the bar a laid-back ambience. Dark red carpeted floor and box beam ceiling completed the decor. The place was another Dick's Hole, some sort of establishment in a little town, but with a more sophisticated interior design.

"Did you order us something?" Grace asked, pointing to the bar behind her.

"Yep. A beer for me and a Midnight Star for you."

She watched me with interest. "What is it?"

"The server described it as a spiked lemonade. With vodka. I thought it was your kind of poison."

"Well, you thought right."

We were on our second round of drinks when Grace's name was announced.

She jumped to her feet, excitement pouring out from her. "How do I look?" she asked, adjusting the red top she was wearing with a pair of dark jeans and ankle boots.

"Perfect." I lifted my bottle of beer. "Go, make me proud," I said with a grin.

A soft blush crept up her cheeks. "I'll try."

Grace exchanged a few words with the guy in charge of the karaoke and walked on the stage. I perused the room. All the eyes were aimed at her. I hadn't been wrong the first time I saw her—she really did possessed a magnetism that was hard to ignore

She waved at me, and we exchanged a smile. My gaze stayed fixed on her, and I hoped—maybe foolishly—that she knew how remarkable I thought she was.

Grace sang her own rendition of Winter Night.

People clapped and sang along.

A genuine smile painted her lips.

She was happy and, in that instant, reminded me of Isla De la Durantaye, the carefree girl I met almost two months ago. Minus the armor.

"How was I?" she asked once she was finished and returned to our table, chugging half of her drink in one go. "Sorry, I was thirsty."

"You were born to rock that stage."

A loud chuckle bubbled out. "Thanks. I had fun, and that's what counts, right? You should have tried. Anyway, a girl gotta pee. I'll be right back."

The second Grace disappeared toward the restrooms, the waitress came back. She dropped her pen right by my feet and made a show of bending forward and pushing her ass against my thigh while she picked it up. She faced me again, toying with the same pen between her lips. "Anything on or off the menu you'd like?"

"Nope. All good."

She traced a long, dark-painted fingertip along my chest. "You sure? I have specials reserved for select customers only. And congratulations, you made the cut."

"As I already said, not interested."

The old me would have relished the idea, but not this new and improved version.

"Want me to change your mind?" She leaned forward, and her lips grazed mine for an infinitesimal second before she whispered next to my ear, "Meet me when you're done."

Whoa, had our roles been reversed and I had acted like that, I'd have been kicked out of this place in two point nine seconds.

"Think about it, handsome."

She turned to leave, swaying her hips and waving at me over her shoulder, when I noticed a frozen Grace ten feet in front of me.

She glared at me, hurt flashing in her brown irises. Raw and almost palpable.

"Wow. Don't be shy on my account." Her clipped words hit me straight in the heart. Where it stung. "Follow her. She's clearly waiting for you to join her behind that door."

She padded forward, drained the rest of her drink, banged the glass on the table, and stormed outside.

I dropped a couple of twenties on the table and scurried after her. "Grace, wait."

She ran into the night, ignoring my pleas.

"It's not what you think. I told her I wasn't into her. Guess she's not smart enough to understand simple words."

Grace halted her escape and spun to face me. "I'm not stupid, Joe. She kissed you. I saw it. Don't deny it happened. Don't paint me as a fool." She flicked her wrist. "Anyway, it's none of my business, so go back in there, and finish what you started. We both know it wouldn't be the first time you fuck a girl you meet in a bar."

"Cheap shot. More so, coming from you."

"I say things as I see them. Stay here. I'm going home."

I blinked. "Home?"

"No. I'm going to cuddle with DH. *That* home."

My shoulders sagged. "Don't go. I have no intention of going back to that bar… Not without you."

She snorted. "I'm not the boss of you. You are free to do whatever or whoever you want, Joe. I'm nobody to you. Just the daughter of the woman your dad married."

Fury swirled in my stomach. "Is that what you believe?"

She folded her arms over her chest. She didn't wear a jacket and would freeze to death if we didn't retreat inside soon. "That's what it is. Don't try to sugarcoat what we are."

"It's not true. Stop making up stories about me when you don't know the truth."

Grace tipped her hip forward. "What's the truth, Joe? Go ahead, enlighten me."

"What do you want me to tell you? That every minute of every day you're on my mind? That nothing in my life has ever felt so right than the night we met and that I was upset when I woke up the next morning and realized you were gone? That I let myself believe you went to grab coffee and would be back because you were in no hurry to leave me? And that I waited three hours before deciding it was a lost cause and you were never coming back? What do you want me to tell you, Grace? We're stuck in a situation that pleases neither of us. And still, we gotta make it work."

Fat tears streamed down her cheeks. "It's not… That's… I don't know what I want you to say, Joe. I wish things were easy. That-that I could fall in love with you and it would…and it would right all the wrongs in the world. In *my* world. I wish I could hold your hand when we're out and about. And kiss you. Because God knows I've been thinking about your kisses and your arms around me for a long fucking time. I wish our parents weren't married, but I-I will always be glad we moved to Pennsylvania because otherwise, you and I might have never met. See how fucked-up this is? We're prisoners in a state of limbo, and I have no idea how to get out of it. Or if I wish to get out of it…"

She wiped her runny nose with the back of her hand.

"All my life, I never belonged. My mom made sure of it. I grew up faster than any kid should. I witnessed my mom making herself sick, thinking she would be loved if she looked a certain way. I saw her cry herself to sleep because she got rejected…again. That only fed her obsessions. She would start a new diet or exercise until she fainted, refusing to eat after sweating at the gym for three hours. Then she would gulp diet and sleeping pills like they were candies. I saw it all. She made me feel ugly and fat because it helped her feel better about herself. She insulted *me*, put *me* on a diet, made *me* exercise, as if it would fix things in *her*. I was forced to be an adult early because my mother would always make herself *the* priority. Her needs always came first. All. The. Freaking. Time. She never once put me first."

"Grace—"

"No. Listen. You're the only person who makes sense in the craziness also called my life. You challenge me. You cheer on me. You make me want to be better, do better, reach for my dreams. You make me want to put my needs first for once. And yet the one thing I desire, I can't have because someone, somewhere, decided it was wrong for us to be together. I'm tired of my mother, society, and everyone around telling me what I should do and how I should do it. Sure, my age on paper says something, but the age in my heart and my soul says something else. I just wish for once their votes would count."

"I-I'm sorry… I should have pushed her away when she got too close."

"No. That's the thing, Joe. You can flirt and kiss or even sleep with whoever you want. You belong to no one, but you. You're free to follow your heart. And be whoever you wanna be. Don't let me or anyone else make you feel bad for going after what you desire. Or anything you wish for."

"I didn't want her. Grace, listen. You gotta believe me. She's not the one my heart is set on. I'm not used to this… To feel stuff. After my mom's death, I-I spent years not caring about anyone else but me. And now I care. I care too fucking much that it scares me. And I'm afraid I'll mess it up."

She used her sleeve to dry her teary eyes. "You can't mess up something that doesn't exist. I wish it did, but when our parents exchanged vows and said *I do*, the choice got stolen from us."

"Don't talk like we don't stand a chance. I don't care about society or our parents… It's we who matter here. Not them. I don't give a shit about their wedding vows."

"Joe, from the start, I lied to you. I made you believe things about me that were false. We never stood a chance."

"I don't agree. I'll prove it to you."

She shook her head. "I'm done with this conversation. I hate fighting with you."

"Well, I'll fight for both of us because I've seen how you look at me. And no matter how much you try to push me away, I won't let you. Not because all I want is to get into your pants, but because I believe in you. Your talents.

Your heart. The girl I've gotten to know amazes me. Every side of her. And I'm proud to be part of her life. Whatever role she'll let me play in it." I turned on my heels. "Come on, I'll drive us home."

She didn't budge.

The chilly night breeze swept across my face.

I removed my hoodie and went back to her, placing it over her shoulders. "Wear this. You're cold."

"Thanks." Her glossy eyes met mine. "I really hate fighting with you."

I draped one arm around her shoulders and pulled her closer. "Me too." I planted a soft kiss on the top of her head.

Thick silence enveloped us as we climbed into the car, the air so charged that if it were a bomb, it would threaten to explode any second.

"If you wanna talk, I'll always be there for you," I said. I glanced at her, but Grace sat motionless in the passenger seat. Defeat shadowed her face, and I despised the fact that I brought it there. At least she had stopped crying after we left Santa's Lodge.

Neither of us spoke as we unlocked the cabin and petted a sleeping DH lying on the couch.

"I'm gonna shower," Grace announced after a while. "I'll see you in the morning."

"Grace—"

She ignored me and went upstairs.

DH nestled in the crook of my elbow. "If only things were simpler..." I buried my fingers in his fur. "I kinda messed up. Not that I did it on purpose. Things are... huh....complicated between Grace and me. She's hurt. *I* hurt her tonight. I didn't mean to. We were doing great even though I'm afraid we were just tiptoeing around the giant elephant standing between us. There are too many obstacles standing in the way of our relationship being simple—most of which are beyond our control. It's just… No matter what we are, I'm not ready to lose her. Once we go back to our lives, we won't see each other anymore. It should make this entire clusterfuck easier, but it won't. How will I be able to protect her from Clarissa if I'm not around?"

DH stared at me.

"I know it's not in my job description, but I've seen the damage that woman can do. Grace will be able to face her, but she gotta learn to love and accept herself fully first." I stretched out on the couch, lying on my back, and placed DH on my chest. "Can you keep a secret? If it were up to me, I would move her to New York with me— just to put as much distance as possible between her and her mom. Until she comes up with a plan. It's silly… Don't tell her, okay? The last thing I want is to freak her out and make this whole situation more complicated than it already is."

DH curled into a ball in the crook of my neck, falling asleep. Scrolling through my phone, I opened the Mistletoe Creek Holiday schedule.

Tomorrow, Lea was organizing an *Eggnog and PJ Breakfast* at the inn. Grace would love that. Right after, there was a *Take a Picture with Your Pet with Santa* photoshoot.

"Hey, DH. On a scale from one to ten, how excited would you be to meet Santa Claus tomorrow?"

He didn't react.

"Yes, I knew you'd be excited."

Around midnight, I went upstairs, ready to go to bed. As I passed Grace's room, I noticed all the lights were off.

"Joe?" Her voice sounded weak in the darkness.

I neared the threshold. "Yeah?"

"I hate when we fight."

I sighed. "I don't like it either. And I don't like it when you're sad. Are we okay, or are you still mad at me?"

She said nothing for a long minute, and I believed she had fallen asleep. Then she replied, "No. None of it is your fault."

"Okay. Good night, Grace."

"Joe?"

"Yes?"

"Can you sleep in here tonight?"

I cleared my throat. "You sure?"

"Sometimes, I-I'm afraid of the dark."

I entered the bedroom and neared the bed. I removed my jeans and my socks but kept my T-shirt on. "Scoot over. I'll watch over you."

On my back under the covers, I opened an arm, and Grace lodged herself against my chest. I brushed her hair back with my fingers. In the dark, all the complications of our lives seemed to fade away.

"Joe? Please don't fall in love with someone else, okay? Not until we untangle the mess we're in."

I swallowed. "Not my intention."

Her breathing evened, and her head grew heavier against my chest.

Once I made sure Grace was fast asleep, I relaxed and surrendered myself to my dreams. Never before had my emotions been so conflicted.

Stardust Inn kitchen overflowed with people this morning. After we woke up entangled together, I told Grace my plans for the day, and she agreed. Now dressed in matching snowman onesie pajamas that we picked up on our way here, we sat at one of the tables. Red tablecloths, white napkins, and golden plates, this was a very chic Christmas brunch. An assortment of pancakes, waffles, eggs, bacon, and grits filled the table. When we first arrived, I asked Lea if she needed help with anything, but she told me to sit back and enjoy the food and company.

A man played Christmas music on the harp in the corner of the room, beside a grand piano. My fingers itched to join him.

Before I could ask Lea if I could maybe join on a song or two, Thomas and Julian, the boys we met at the tree lighting ceremony a week ago and who were sitting at a far table, waved in our direction. "Look, Mama. It's the pretty princess," Thomas said, pointing at Grace. "Can we go say hi?"

Their mother said something, and they both nodded. They jumped to their feet, but she called out a warning before they could get too far. "Careful, don't run and break any of Lea's snow globes, boys."

I turned around, and that was when I noticed the display of snow globes on the shelves behind us. Dozens of them.

"We won't," Julian said, grabbing his little brother's hand.

"Hey, guys. How is it going?" Grace greeted them, scooting closer to me on the bench to leave room for them beside her.

"Awesome," Julian said. "We built ornaments with stuff we found in the recycle bin yesterday, and we're going to the ice-skating rink later today. Did you visit the castle?"

"Yes, we went to see what the fuss was all about last week," I said. "You were right, guys. It's pretty cool."

"Are you gonna take part in the gingerbread contest next week? Last year, we finished first in the little kids' category. This year we're big kids, so we're gonna decorate a house with icing and candies."

"I'd love to go." Grace smiled. "Will you team up with me, Joe?"

"Anytime, princess."

Their mom gestured for them to join her.

"Guys, I think you're requested over there." I pointed in the direction of the table they had occupied minutes ago.

"Gotta go," Julian said. "Come on, Thomas, Mama needs us."

"Bye, Grace. Bye, Joe."

"Still adorable," I said once they left. "Can you keep my seat warm while I'm gone?" I asked Grace.

"Sure… Huh, where are you going?"

I kissed her forehead before I could realize what I was doing. "You'll see."

I met with Lea, who accepted my proposal to play the piano.

Grace's eyes widened the moment she spotted me at the piano, rolling my sleeves, and wiggling my fingers in anticipation.

Once the harp player finished the song, I leaned in, and we agreed on a playlist.

Playing the piano had always been as easy as breathing for me. When I was six, I visited one of my mother's friends who taught music at the university. I sat in front of the black and white keys and knew exactly how to play.

The keys felt like home as my fingers glided over them.

People in the dining room started to sing. Thomas and Julian and three little girls came to sit cross-legged on the floor in front of me, watching, wondrous expressions illuminating their faces.

I couldn't reel in my grin. I was in my element right now. And I enjoyed every second of it.

From the way Grace stared at me with some sort of admiration, I thanked life for putting her on my road.

I finished my set and returned to my breakfast.

"Your talent blows my mind," Grace whispered as I filled my plate with eggs and bacon. "I had an idea you were skilled, because duh…you play on Broadway. But this was beyond all my expectations."

"Thanks. Guess we're both gifted in our own way."

"You are." She fidgeted with a spoon on the table, and I grabbed her hand to still her movements.

"Hey, you are too. No matter what you choose to do, Grace, I have a feeling you'll do great."

"You really think so?"

"I'm sure of it."

We finished eating, chatting with the people sitting across from us. A couple in their late twenties and a single dad of a teenage boy.

Later, Lea clapped her hands, demanding attention. "Thank you all for coming to our annual *Eggnog and PJ Breakfast*. I hope you all enjoyed it. For those of you who are interested, we'll have the first edition of the *Holly Jolly Scavenger Hunt* on Friday night. I hope to see you there. Now, you're all dismissed. Go enjoy the rest of your day. Don't worry about cleaning up. I have a team of Santa's elves ready to tackle the dishes." As if on cue, five guys dressed as elves exited the kitchen door, and everyone started laughing.

"Mistletoe Creek residents never do anything half-ass," Grace said.

"Nope. Come on, let's go to our first family outing. I'm sure DH can't wait to sit on Santa's lap."

"We'll make family Christmas cards. I think we should stay in our PJs."

"Your wishes are my orders," I teased with a wink.

And just like that, we became the *non-couple* couple, dressed in matching outfits, who took their kitten for a family Christmas portrait.

Now I was certain Anderson would never believe me unless I sent him one of these pictures.

Never before would I have imagined myself parading through town dressed as a snowman and waiting in line at the pet store to see Santa with a kitten, but here I was.

This new version of me was nothing like the previous one, where I was a carefree bachelor, but I was beginning to like him a lot.

Chapter 11

Grace

The next two weeks passed in a blur. In between strolling around town and entering Christmas-themed activities, Joe and I were busy.

I knew he had talked with Philip twice and promised his father we were doing fine.

I mostly worked on schoolwork during the day, and at night, when we stayed in, we played board games or watched some TV by the fireplace, DH nestled in the middle, forcing us apart. When we went out, we explored the town or drove around for hours just for the pleasure of discovering new places we'd never visited before.

So far, Joe and I had been good at keeping things platonic between us. We had learned to stop touching each other and always stayed at least two feet apart. And until now, it had worked fine.

"Are you ready to win?" I asked him as we sat on opposite sides of our designated table for the *Gingerbread Deco-rating Contest*.

"I never lose, baby."

I had no idea if it was a slip of the tongue or Joe really meant to call me *baby*, but no matter what, it sent a zing through me. Everyone in town thought we were dating, and neither of us ever took the time to deny it. We just rolled with it and embraced the anonymity this town offered. Like in that bar the night we met, we could be anyone we wanted to be here. Damn the consequences.

Status of our relationship: undefined.

"I'm in charge of the icing," I said.

"You are?"

"Yep. This white thing can't resist me. I'll put so much of it, filling every crack that our house will never collapse. And then I'll eat whatever is left because it tastes delicious."

"And what will you do when you get that white stuff all over your hands? Please enlighten me."

"I'll lick it clean. I wasn't allowed icing when I was little. I need to make the most of it while I can. It's my birthday soon. I deserve a treat." I dipped a finger into the bowl in front of me and brought it to my mouth as if to prove a point. With swirls of my tongue, I clean my digit. "See? All good now. Not even sticky."

Joe said nothing, and when I met his gaze, he appeared like he was about to eat me up alive.

I melted a little in my seat.

He swept his lips with his tongue in slow motion, and I got entranced by the movement.

Why wasn't he looking away?

"Are you all right? What's going on?"

He shook his head, his pupils dilated, as we faced each

other. "Grace, you have a fucking dirty mouth, and you're not even aware."

"Oh…" Everything I just said bounced back inside my head. I cupped my mouth. "Oops."

"Yeah." He brought his forefinger and thumb close together. "I'm this close to blowing a gasket. You are driving me nuts. And it's a dangerous territory you're entering."

"I didn't… I was… Well, I thought—"

The man with the microphone, standing in front of the small room, cut us off.

"Ladies and gentlemen, welcome to our annual *Gingerbread Decorating Contest*. Each team has everything they might need in front of them. Cookies, house parts, icing, candies. You have one hour to come up with the most incredible designs. Are you ready?"

Everyone said "*Yes*".

"You know how lucky I am to be teamed up with a future designer, right?" Joe asked.

"I thought it was because of my filthy mouth." My cheeks warmed up as I held his heavy gaze.

"Yeah. That too." He paused. "I was thinking… You should apply to fashion school next year. I saw how talented you were when you modified that gown. Just sayin'."

"You think I'm talented?"

He nodded. "More than you give yourself credit for."

"My mom… She will never agree. She says I should go into business or medicine because, according to her, I can't be a model since I'm plus-size. She said I have a crappy sense of fashion."

"Sorry, but that woman is a witch. Don't listen to a word she says because it's probably false."

I shrugged. "I figured out a long time ago that I could only count on myself if I wanted to be happy."

"You can count on me too. I won't let you down."

A new surge of heat crept up my face. "You don't have to say that."

"I know. I mean it, though. There's more than one way to be successful in the fashion industry. Too bad Clarissa missed the lesson."

We worked side by side for over thirty minutes, Joe icing gingerbread man and woman cookies while I decorated the house.

"And Grace?"

"Yes." We both froze, facing each other. "Never say you're plus-size again. Embrace who you are and fuck your mom or whatever the industry dictates. You are the most beautiful girl I've ever met. And believe me, going to arts school, I've met quite a few. From anorexic ballerinas to entitled wannabe actresses. Don't lose that light you possess. Nobody can steal it from you if you don't give them the power to do it."

Emotions lodged in my chest. "You really mean it?"

"Every word."

Joe and I finished in second place after the jury crowned two middle-aged women as the winning team. As a second-place prize, we won a dinner for two at The Woodsman, an upscale grill slash tavern in town.

Julian and Thomas finished third amongst the older kids. They both received Christmas socks filled with goodies, and by the sight of their huge smiles, they couldn't be happier. We congratulated them before they ran away to show their friends.

"I told you we'd win," I said as we drove back to the cabin to shower and change.

"I told you I never lose," Joe said.

Why did all his words sound like dirty promises? I had to stop imagining us under the sheets pleasuring each other with our mouths. We were past that, and still, my body and mind couldn't get onboard with this new plan concerning us.

Joe ordered wine and poured me some. "To us." He lifted his glass, and I clinked it with mine.

"To us," I echoed.

The Woodsman was the fanciest restaurant in Mistletoe Creek. It had a warm and cozy atmosphere. Bronze wallpaper with dark furniture, a patterned carpet covering most of the wooden floor, and a stoned fireplace. Brick walls covered in ivy gave the exterior a timeless look. Inside and out, the place had a castle-like atmosphere.

"Thought about what I said earlier?" Joe asked.

I tipped a brow at him.

"About your college application?"

I nodded, feeling flushed, unsure whether it was from the attention he gave me or the alcohol buzzing in my veins, spreading warmth across my face. "Earlier, when you were showering, I researched colleges. New York Fashion Institute has the best program." There, I said it. The first step toward my freedom.

"You did?"

"Yep." I swirled the wine in my glass. I didn't know why I suddenly felt shy while talking about my future.

"I thought when I shower, you picture me naked." His face remained stoic as he spoke the words.

"Joe." I fanned myself with my napkin.

"Just kidding. I love it when you blush. You look cute as hell." He extended his arm over the table to cover my hand with his. "Sorry. For NYFI, anything specific you need to do to apply?"

"A portfolio. And they say creativity is the key. I was thinking… Never mind, it's silly."

"Tell me." He squeezed my hand, and just then I realized he never let go.

"What if I send them a real-life portfolio? Pieces of clothing I designed and sewed. The real thing. I could create three pieces, and the rest could be a digital portfolio. What do you think? Does it sound doable or crazy?"

He blinked a few times. "That is genius. I love the idea. If you succeed in putting it together in time, it's going to be a success for sure. What can I do to help?"

I let out a laugh. "Don't get ahead of yourself. I haven't had the chance to think about it fully. You spun the idea on me this afternoon. I need to do more research first."

"We're doing it. I see the light in your eyes. You love the idea. You came alive just now when you told me about it."

"If I wanna be ready in time, I should start working on pieces soon. I need to do a few to be able to select the three winners."

"Tomorrow. We'll set everything up in the empty bedroom. I'll be your assistant. Whatever you need, I'll provide."

"Why does that sound like sex promises?" I teased, sipping on my wine.

"For once, it's not. And don't tempt me to turn it into one. I was thinking of being your model. Are you going to design men's or women's pieces? I can also pose naked if it helps with your creative juice. I'm not judging. Every artist has a different process."

I threw my napkin at him over the table. "You're such a pig."

"You didn't complain that one time."

Now I bet my face was bright pink.

We ordered copious amounts of food, the conversation flowing easily between us. I basked in a boozy bliss, enjoying the company a little too much.

"Will you ever tell me why our cat is named DH?" I asked between bites.

"Nah." Amusement danced in Joe's eyes. "Not until you guess it." He sipped on his wine, studying me. I could tell we'd have to take a cab to go back to the cabin tonight, neither of us sober enough to drive.

I rested my chin on my hand. "It's not fair. It could be anything."

He shrugged. "Take a guess."

"Nah. I'll wait until I'm confident I can get it right."

"Suit yourself. Ready to go?"

I nodded.

I linked my arm with Joe's as we waited for the car to pick us up. "You wanna know what I'm wishing for?"

"Tell me."

"That you would kiss me goodnight." I felt strong enough to speak the words I had locked inside. "Tonight feels like a real date. It's perfect."

"Want to know what I'm wishing for?"

I nodded. The winter breeze sweeping across my face cooled off some of the arousal spreading inside me.

"I wish I could cherish every inch of your flesh with my tongue, my hands, and my dick."

Neither of us looked elsewhere, as if we were cast under a spell. I yearned to draw Joe's chin dimple with my finger. To rake my hands through his tousled hair. To feel his lips claiming mine in a slow torturous kiss.

I bet he could read my thoughts because he erased the

distance between us, his body flush against mine. So much that I could feel his heartbeat through my chest.

Without a word, he tucked strands of my hair behind my ear.

We remained still, our gazes never faltering.

"Grace, if you could see yourself the way I do, never again would you doubt yourself." He swallowed, the bob of his throat hypnotizing me, before stepping away and stealing every particle of air from my lungs.

That night, I tossed and turned for what felt like hours.

Joe's words replayed in my head on a loop.

I wish I could cherish every inch of your flesh with my tongue, my hands, and my dick.

If you could see yourself the way I do, never again would you doubt yourself.

Unable to find a soothing position or abandon myself to sleep, I pushed my hand under the waistband of my panties, the T-shirt—Joe's shirt I stole that morning—bunching at my waist as I caressed myself the way I dreamed he would do. The way I remembered him doing. And just after I exploded in a climax and was drifting to sleep, I heard a muffled grunt coming from the other side of the wall.

Maybe I wasn't the only one unable to fall asleep tonight.

Chapter 12
Grace

Joe and I were sitting on the couch, watching a movie on the screen mounted on the wall.

"Girl, why do I feel like every Christmas movie you've made me watch since we moved in is the same but with different characters? The plots are similar, the scenes predictable, the storyline too much alike to be a coincidence. When you've seen one, you've seen them all."

I sighed. "Stop complaining. Nobody said Christmas movies have to be blockbusters with stunts and a complicated plot. Most are just copies of each other, but I don't know… Somehow, it works. It's supposed to be all about love, hope, and redemption. They fill that purpose."

"I went to art school. We had movie classes. None of the teachers would have passed a student who had come up with such an excuse for a story. Cinema is fun when it's entertaining, surprising, and one of a kind. These movies fail on at least two of those fronts. I just don't see the appeal."

"You never watched holiday rom-coms in the past?" My jaw hung open at this piece of information.

"When I was a kid, I watched classics with my mom every Christmas Eve. Then I became a teenager and watched those edgier Christmas-themed movies. With the catastrophes, epic booze-induced parties, plane hijackings. Those kinds of movies. They are still Christmas movies. Just more entertaining and less predictable than what we're watching right now."

"And how exactly are plane hijacking thrillers supposed to put you in a festive mood? How are they supposed to inject you with hope that everything will be all right and that love will always win?"

"Because. The hero wins and then gets to his kids just in time before they wake up on Christmas morning after he saved the world." Joe's eyes lit up as he spoke. "In my opinion, it's much more hopeful than the CEO going to the countryside to dismantle a family farm only to fall for their daughter, the typical heroine who never wears heels and drives a tractor and whose only friends are cows. Those are clichés."

I shrugged. "Maybe I like clichés. What's wrong about them?"

"Nothing. I just think people in Hollywood could make them a bit more interesting. They would attract a much bigger audience if they got, first, better funding, and second, some substance to make them more exciting. They can keep the formula if it works but could take it to a new level. Just a thought."

I blew out a full breath. "I'm not saying you're wrong. I understand why after three movies on the same night, you might get bored—and for the record, I'm not admitting you're right—as they all sound alike." I turned off the television. "Let's do something else."

"I checked the town calendar. There's nothing planned at this hour tonight." Joe unlocked his phone and flipped it so I could see the screen.

"But we could do some caroling."

He coughed, and I believed, for a second, he would choke on his saliva. "You're kidding, right?"

"No. This will be fun." I stood and tugged at his hand. "Come on, Mr. *I Judge Christmas Movies*. The town center is where the fun stuff happens."

"Grace, you're serious?"

"Yes." I released his hand and hurried toward the stairs. "Last one who's ready is on litter box duty for a week."

Before I could reach the landing, strong arms wrapped around my waist and lifted me up. I laughed my heart out, trying to escape his iron grip. Before I could understand what Joe was doing, he scooted me over his shoulder, padded to his room, and dropped me on his bed.

"What are you—?"

He watched me with a funny expression that dissipated as quickly as it came. "Making sure you're not getting ready first."

"But—"

"No but. You can't escape this room, or I'll bring you back here. Only when I'm ready, you'll go change."

I kneeled on the mattress. "Not fair. That's not how it works." I threw a pillow at him, but he dodged it, and it landed on the floor. "The rules don't say you're allowed to kidnap me."

"And who made the rules, Grace?"

"Me. I did."

"Well, I think it's about time I take charge and make the rules from now on."

I shook my head. "No. I don't agree."

He waggled his eyebrows. "Too bad. I think you in my bedroom is fitting, and…huh… And nothing." He pinched the fabric of his T-shirt at the nape of his neck and peeled it off, offering me a full view of his chiseled chest before turning toward the dresser.

I used the distraction to spring forward and jump on his back, locking my arms and legs around him like a monkey. "See? I'm not easily *kidnappable*. You stand no chance. I'll fight until my last breath. And I've decided you're the one on litter duty."

In a swift movement, Joe flipped me in his arms. He turned and threw me onto the bed, my back hitting the mattress with a bounce. As he hovered over me, shirtless, I used all my inner power not to ogle him like I yearned to.

"Grace, the thing is… I'm the kind of guy who enjoys power in the bedroom. And right now, you're lying on *my* bed. Which means, I'm in charge."

Shivers traversed my body.

Joe lowered himself over me, our chests almost brushing as we both breathed fast.

His pupils dilated, and a hunter's glare appeared in his eyes. One that aroused every cell in my body.

He licked his lips, and I almost combusted underneath him.

For once, I wanted him to take charge. The one time we slept together, I never relented the power to him. I fought him the entire time. It wasn't passion we shared that night, but a raw, animalistic hunger for each other.

Right now, though, I craved the dominance he'd hinted at. I ached for him to take me however he wanted.

My lips parted on an exhale.

Gosh, all I wished for was his mouth cherishing mine and other sensitive parts of my body that throbbed for him, and for his hands to roam over my naked flesh.

Joe closed some of the gap separating our bodies.

His breath fanned my face.

In that instant, I lost touch with everything around me.

All I could see, smell, feel was him. Even though we were still too far apart.

His nose traced the length of mine.

My heart rate went ballistic.

I stared at the quickening pulse in his neck.

His palms molded to mine, and he brought my arms over my head.

This was it. Our *Fuck you* to society and taking back the control of our lives. Of our hearts' desires.

"Joe—" My voice sounded weaker than intended. When he watched me like a starving man, I didn't have the willpower to resist him.

I threw my head back, lengthening my neck so he could devour it unrestrained, with no barriers between us.

My breasts swelled.

Weeks of tiptoeing around each other made that instant even more exciting. I could no longer fight the desires stirring in my body and my heart.

Joe knitted his fingers through mine, holding me still. I had become his prisoner and relished every second of it.

"Make me yours," I pleaded in a low voice. "Please." Liquid desire pooled in my lower belly. I was about to melt, and he hadn't even undressed me yet.

Joe and I, we were two opposite poles of a magnet unable to resist the other's pull.

He leaned over me, and I felt the hard part of him rubbing against my thigh. His lips skimmed over mine. I was dying. I needed more, but a part of me waited anxiously for his next move.

With one swift movement, as if electrocuted, he jumped back and blinked, releasing his grip on my hands. "Fuck. I can't… We can't…"

His rejection felt like a dagger to my heart. Even though I knew he was right.

Trying to hide the hurt I felt, I raised myself up, leaning on my elbows, while he stood at the end of the bed, putting more distance between us. "What if I want you to?"

He raked a hand through his tousled blond locks. "That's not how it works, Grace."

"There's no one but us here. Nobody will snitch on us. Please. We both need this. You can't deny our undeniable connection…our blazing chemistry… In fact, I'm pretty sure the whole town can feel it."

"It's not about what *I* want. It's about doing what's right. And us…this… It can't happen. *We* can't happen. It would be wrong."

"Wrong for whom?"

"I'm not having this talk with you. You should go change now. I'll be on litter duty all week. I'm sorry. I'm the one who put us in this situation. I won't do it again."

"Are you listening to yourself? You're talking as if you tried to kill me."

He remained silent, turning his back on me.

I jumped to my feet, standing behind him, as red-hot fury boiled inside me. "Go ahead. Avoid looking at me. That's very mature of you."

He flinched at my accusations, tension rolling down his stiff back. His arms hung at his sides, and he fisted his hands.

I waited, but he didn't acknowledge me, so I continued

to talk, unable to stop spilling the words weighing heavy on my heart. "Well, I never pictured you as a coward, Joe Crawford. You're all hot for a second, and then you're cold as ice. I'm not doing this dance with you anymore. It's not healthy for anyone involved. I won't let you play with my heart for another second."

He twirled around, grabbed my wrists, and walked me until my back rested against the wall. "Coward? You think being reasonable is the same as being a chickenshit? News flash, Grace. Some of us can't afford to get in trouble with the law. I have my life to think of, my father, my job. I'm not willing to risk it for a quick romp in the sheets."

My head hit the wall as if he had stabbed me. "A quick romp in the sheets? Is that all I am to you?"

He avoided my eyes, looking in the distance.

"Answer the question, Joe. Am I only a fuck to you?"

"I'm not answering that."

"I'm withdrawing the invitation. Tonight, I'm going caroling. Alone."

"No."

"Yes. I need space…from you. And don't try to stop me."

Chapter 13

I checked the time for the umpteenth time. It was almost two in the morning and still no sign of Grace. All my calls had been going straight to voicemail, and my texts left unanswered.

I should have never seduced her earlier. It was a rookie mistake. She looked so hot and enticing, spread on my bed, that I had trouble resisting and let my dick lead the way. Stupid me blurred the lines even more than they already were. This time, I might have screwed up our relationship beyond repair. Grace wasn't a toy I could play with or some nameless girl I could fuck and forget all about the next morning.

She lived under my skin—every minute of every day—and it messed with my composure. And with my common sense.

I almost did something I knew I would regret later, and now she had chosen to push me away.

Fucking amazing.

Why was I still hung up on her after all this time? I should already be over her. Stupid heart, it got involved when it should have stayed out of the equation.

Not convinced my calls and messages were going through, I checked once again to see if my phone's ringtone was turned on. I knew I was being lame, yet I couldn't seem to stop.

I fidgeted with my phone, unsure what to do and trying not to give in to the temptation. But weakness got the better of me, and I hit dial. Voicemail.

This was becoming ridiculous.

She shouldn't be allowed to stay out this late.

Fuck, I wasn't the boss of her.

What if something happened to her?

What if she got lost?

The girl was driving me insane.

She said she needed space, but how much time did she need?

Nobody was caroling at two in the morning.

Where was she now?

Maybe she got into trouble. Maybe something happened.

I tried to tell myself she was fine. That she'd find her way back. That she was okay.

But the silence stretching around me said otherwise.

On my feet, I paced the living room. I should drive around town. Find her. But if she came back while I was out, I'd worry while she was safe and sound.

Fuck my life.

My hand buzzed, and it took me a moment to realize my phone was vibrating in my palm. *Unknown number.*

"Hi."

Loud music played in the background, and I heard voices. "Is…is this Joe?"

"Yeah. Speaking."

"Hi, this is, huh…Lea from the Stardust Inn. I-I think *youuu* should pick up Grace. She's pretty wasted. We…we were drinking…" A hiccup. "*Annnd* soon we were both drunk. Anyway, I think *youuu* should come and get her."

Drunk. Yeah, Grace's answer to fights. Of all the scenarios I'd played out in my head, this was the one I didn't expect. A *déjà vu*. As if getting loaded could fix all her problems.

"Coming. Where are you?"

"Sa…sl…g…e." Was the line bad, or was Lea too out of it to speak coherent words?

Clenching and unclenching my other hand, I tried to keep calm.

"Lea, I can't hear you. Where are you guys?"

"*Sorry*, I got distracted. Santa's Lodge. It-it's karaoke night, *annnd* Grace is rocking the stage."

"I'll be there in ten minutes."

Grabbing my key and wallet, I hauled myself behind the wheel. I focused on the road, and the darkness's low visibility helped keep my anger in check.

I entered Santa's Lodge, scanning the place, looking for a blonde girl whose act of rebellion had knotted my insides with fear all night.

As if we were in sync, our gazes locked from a distance.

My heart pounded in my chest.

Grace turned her head, dismissing me with a glance, then returned to the song she was singing.

When did she change? When she left earlier, she was wearing jeans and a sweater. Now she was wearing a tiny red dress and a Santa hat. I didn't miss the way the patrons' eyes undressed her. *Yeah, guys, get in line.*

Lea met me before I could reach the stage.

"*Hiii*, Joe," she singsonged. "*Youuu* came?" Her cheeks were flushed and her eyes, shiny.

"What's going on?" I pointed to the stage. "How did this happen?"

"Grace *annnd* I caroled together for a…for a while, and when she…huh…suggested *thaaat* we go for a drink, I, well, I thought it was a *goood* idea. We ended up here, *annnd* the cocktails kept coming. I-I have to go home, and I didn't want Grace to be…to be all alone. I thought we could share a car, *buuut* she refuses to leave."

"Thanks, I'll take care of it from here. You okay to get a ride?"

"*Yesss*. Rose is picking me up. *Alll* fine."

I nodded. "Fine. Thanks for calling me."

"*Annnd* Joe? Fair warning. She's…huh…mad at *youuu*. Said you don't *lovvve* her."

I sighed. "Thanks for the heads-up."

She left, and I stood still for a short beat, watching Grace sing in her too-short, naughty Mrs. Claus dress.

The song ended, and she lifted her drink above her head, people cheering as she downed it in one go.

"Party's over," I said, nearing the stage.

"No. It's *ovvver* when I say it's *ovvver*," Grace argued, slurring her words.

"Let's go home." I motioned to grab her hand, but she stepped back.

"*Nooo*. I'm *chooosing* to be here, and *youuu* don't have a say in my *wheredouts*…huh…no. My *whereitsout*." She squinted, as if trying to gather her thoughts. "*Myyy* whereabouts. *Yesss*, whereabouts." She smiled proudly. "Go back to bed, and let *meee* be."

"Not how it works. Sorry to disappoint you."

She lifted a finger. "It's *almossst* my birth"—hiccup

—"day. I'm allowed to…to drink and to… Huh, what was I saying? Oh *yesss*, I'm allowed to fuck F.U.C.K. whoever I-I want because I'm an adult *annnd* I make my own decisions. All. Of. Them. Do *youuu* hear me, Joe? I am…I am the boss of me. Not *youuu*, not my mom. *Meee*."

I inched closer and looped one arm around her waist. "Lean on me. I have you."

"*Nooo*. You don't *under…stand*. And you-you are not listening. *Youuu're* not allowed to touch me. It always *hurtsss* me afterward, and I-I don't want to be sad because, Joe, you make *meee* sad. Super sad. S.A.D. *Annnd* happy too. Like you are the sun in *myyy* sky. But also, *verrry* sad when *youuu* push me away."

"It was never my intention."

"Same result. I'm *ovvver* you now. You didn't deny I was…huh…I was only a fuck to *youuu*."

"I didn't mean it. Grace, our relationship confuses me too."

"It-it doesn't matter anymore. Even if *youuu* try to seduce S.E.D.U.C.E. me, I won't fall for it. *Weee* are done. D.O.N.E."

I watched her with amusement. "Okay, you like to spell words tonight."

"Only trying to make sure I-I'm being *cleaaar*. Done."

"For what it's worth, I'm glad you didn't take the car tonight so I could come to pick you up."

"The roads are *dangerooous*. Super steep and dark. The last thing I…I want"—she lifted a finger—"is to end up in a ditch. D.I.T.C.H. It was my *decisionnn*. I-I'm an adult, so I *deciddde* my *decisionnns*. Okay?"

A soft laugh exited my mouth. "Yeah. An adult. Who decides her own decisions. Got it."

"Glad you…*youuu're* not arguing with me." She nodded. And nodded again. "You won't affect *meee* anymore, Joe Crawford. *Nevvver*. I will not give *youuu* the power to do it." She turned to face me as I led her outside. "Say you *agreee* with me."

"Okay."

"*Goood*."

We arrived at the cabin, and Grace started rummaging through the refrigerator while I packed the fireplace. "I'm *superrr* hungry. Where's the food?" she asked, popping blueberries into her mouth. This was a different version of drunk-Grace tonight. Nothing like the happy-no-worries version of her I met when we were at Dick's Hole. "Ramen. *Yesss*. Ramen would taste *sooo* good right now."

"You're a hungry drunk, aren't you?"

"*Nopppe*. I'm not drunk."

"You're not?"

She shook her head multiple times. "Joe, *youuu're* making things up. *Stoppp*. I'm still mad at *youuu*. I'm hungry. Period. P.E.R.I.O.D."

I snickered at her antics.

Turning her back to me, Grace bent forward, opened a cupboard, and took a pot out.

I joined her and tried to remove it from her hands. "You're not playing with hot water. Gimme that." I opened my palm, but she hid the pot behind her back. "Grace. Please. You are an adult, and you decide your decisions, but I'll take care of the hot water for now, okay?"

She huffed a long breath. "O-okay."

I led her to the living room and put one of the Christmas movies she liked on the television. I grabbed a blanket and a sleepy DH. "Here. Relax while I cook for you."

"Will *youuu* make ramen soup?"

"Yes."

I placed DH on her lap once she sat down, and Grace snuggled with him. "*Thannnk* you."

I shoved my hands in my pockets and bobbed my head once. "You're welcome."

I was itching to tell her she didn't have to get drunk when things didn't go her way and that avoiding me wasn't the solution to our disagreement. But now wasn't the time, so I decided to let it go.

When I returned to the living room with two bowls of soup on a tray, Grace had fallen asleep, the kitten nestled against her chest. The sight of them drew a smile on my lips.

I lifted her legs, slid under them, and ate while watching the rest of the movie.

Two strangers bumping into each other in a super-market aisle. A single billionaire dad and a homeless woman. Things were easy between them. Nobody judged them for falling in love, no matter how impossible their relationship appeared to be.

"You wanna know a secret, Grace?" I asked her sleepy figure. "It's not that I don't love you or that I don't want you, because God knows I do. I'm just too chickenshit to admit it to you. Happy now? You were right. I'm scared of what we could be." I set the tray beside me and massaged her feet. She shifted in her sleep, mumbling something I couldn't understand, a faint smile tugging at her lips. "One day I will be brave enough, and I hope it won't be too late then."

My back hurt from the uncomfortable position I slept in. With my hands, I massaged my shoulders in an attempt to remove the knots that were lodged there.

"Good, you're awake. Morning, sleepyhead."

"Grace?" I cracked my eyes open, searching for the source of her voice.

She sat next to me on the couch, tying her sneakers.

Couch?

I scratched my temple. "We slept here?"

She shrugged. "Guess I fell asleep, and you followed suit. I have very foggy memories of last night."

"I picked you up at Santa's Lodge after you went on a drinking spree with Lea. Then you were hungry. I made you ramen soup, but you were out cold before it was even ready."

"You cooked for me? In the middle of the night?"

I moved to a sitting position. "No big deal."

"Joe, it *is* a big deal. You cooked for me, and I didn't even stay awake long enough to enjoy it."

"There's leftover in the fridge."

Her lips thinned. "Thanks. I appreciate it." She breathed out, and her easy smile returned. "Now get up and put some shoes on. We're going out."

I rubbed a hand over my face to erase the last traces of sleep tightening my features. "Going where?" I checked the time on my phone. "It's not even nine o'clock yet."

"It's snowing."

"It is?"

"Yes. And I wanna make the most of it. Hurry."

She opened the door and ran outside before I could even move to my feet.

At the front door, I rested my shoulder against the doorjamb, enjoying the sight as Grace twirled around, trying to catch snowflakes with her tongue. My lips curled up of their own volition. "Have you never seen snow in your life?"

She stopped spinning to stare at me. "I'm from Texas, Joe. Snow isn't a common occurrence."

"You love?"

"No, I adore. It's beautiful. What are you waiting for? Put some shoes on. We have a full day ahead of us."

"What's on the schedule?"

"Snowmen, snow angels, snowball fights, snow sculptures, snowshoes. Everything snow." She frowned when her eyes landed on me. "Why aren't you excited? It's a snow day. It'll be fun. Trust me."

"Girl, I trust you, but there's not enough snow to do any of those things. You need at least an inch, if not more."

"Oh. You sure?" Her face fell.

"Huh…sorry?" My answer sounded more like a question than an affirmation.

"It's still beautiful, though." She surveyed the not-quite white scenery. "Can I watch it fall?"

"You wanna watch the snow fall? From the window?"

"Yeah. Is that a thing? Watching the snowstorm from inside?"

"Snowstorm? Nah. These are just a few snowflakes. Nothing like a storm."

"Oh." She looked defeated. "I like the snow. It brings me peace. What else do people do when it snows outside?"

"You want to experience a real snow day?"

"Yes." Joy returned to her face.

"Okay, that we can do," I said. "Let's make hot chocolate, bake cookies, put Christmas music on, change into our PJs, and pretend we're snowed in."

Sparks shone in her eyes. "And we're stuck in a cabin in the woods?"

"That's the idea."

"Perfect." Her entire face lit up, and her contagious energy rubbed off on me. "I love it. I'll put music on, and you boil the water."

Thirty minutes later, we put a batch of molasses cookies into the oven.

"Joe?"

"Yeah?"

"I like playing house with you. It feels like the kind of day the kid in me should have experienced growing up. Did you do that with your mom? Bake and spend a day in pajamas?"

"I did. On Christmas Day, we always spent the day baking and playing outside when it snowed. We would visit my grandparents and listen to music all day, dancing and singing."

"How was she?"

"My mom?"

"Yeah."

I hadn't talked about my mother to anyone in a long time. "Pretty. Big eyes, high cheekbones. Her hair was the same color as mine. She always smiled, like her world was the happiest place on Earth. I miss her." A surge of emotions washed through me. "Thanks for asking. Not a lot of people do." I remained silent for a moment. "In many ways, you remind me of her. Your eyes. And your heart."

"I wish I could have met her."

"She would have loved you." I took a big inhale. "Enough with the trip down memory lane. Pick a movie. I'll make some popcorn. I'm gonna give you the best snow day you've ever had."

We sat beside each other, snacking, while the opening scene of a Christmas action movie played on the screen.

"You didn't wanna watch one of your rom-coms?" I asked Grace.

"Nah. I thought we could do it your way this time."

"Thanks." I draped an arm over the backrest of the couch, and after a while, Grace leaned against me.

She made me feel stuff I had locked deep inside years ago. She made me feel whole. And calm.

For the first time since my mother died, I felt like love could maybe be an integral part of my life. I was done chasing it away.

All my doubts left me, and I relaxed against her.

Grace cocked her head, and our eyes fused. The smile she aimed at me filled me with hope. "Joe, this is the best snow day ever. I'm happy that my first time is with you."

I planted a kiss on her forehead. "I'm glad we're doing this together."

She repositioned her head, and I pulled her in.

And for the next few hours, life outside the gingerbread house didn't exist.

Chapter 14

Joe

DH rubbed against my leg. "Just a sec, little one. I wanna finish prepping dinner before your mama comes down. She's been working all day on her college application project." Yes, Grace didn't care it was Christmas Eve tonight. We even refused to partake in the town *PJ and Movie Marathon* earlier because she wanted to finish the dress she was working on before the New Year. Our kitten purred, and I bent down to pat his head. "She's determined. I love that about her. I'm glad she's finding her voice. Are you excited for our first Christmas together? I hope the turkey tastes good. I have never baked one before, but your mama once said she likes it, and since it's her birthday in a few hours, I want to make her happy."

I lit a dozen candles around the main floor, giving the place a romantic atmosphere.

Tonight, I would be honest with Grace. Jitters filled my stomach at the mere thought of opening up to her about my feelings. I had no idea if she'd be willing to give us a chance since I'd been pushing her away every time attraction took us hostage. I could count far more reasons why we shouldn't be together than why we should even try.

We'd been stuck in this tug-of-war for weeks now. Since our fight last weekend when she left and ended up wasted, I did a lot of thinking. I was done with the invisible barriers I'd erected in my head and around my heart. Grace was right when she accused me of leading her on and being all hot and cold. I wanted it all this time, and I wouldn't let my fears seep in and control my actions anymore. No more leading her on. Either way, I couldn't hide how I felt any longer. I just hoped she would reciprocate my feelings and not give me a taste of my own medicine by rejecting me.

I added logs into the fireplace when two arms wrapped around me from behind, stopping me before I could put the screen back. "You know who's gonna be eighteen in less than three hours? And free from their mother?"

I whirled around and dropped a kiss on her forehead. "You ready to claim your independence? I've been thinking about it… When we go back to Silverville, we should talk about you mov—"

A knock on the door cut our discussion short. I shut my eyes and took a deep breath through my nose to quiet my annoyance. Whoever stood on the other side of the door had a wicked sense of timing.

"You're expecting someone?" Grace asked.

"Nope. I'll go and see who it is. This conversation isn't over. Can you feed DH?"

"Sure."

I watched her fetch kibbles from a bag and serve it to our fur baby.

"You hungry, you?" She always used a baby voice to

address him. "Come on, let's get some yummy food into your tiny belly."

I shook my head, unable to stop grinning when I unlocked the door and yanked it open. My humor died instantly. Tension washed through my entire being, and I clamped the edge of the door with my fingers. The last person I thought I'd ever see stood there, dressed to impress, as if she had just stepped off the runway, her signature plastic smile anchored to her face. "Clarissa, what are you doing here?" My tone was clipped, uninviting, and filled with disdain.

"Hi, Joe. You're not happy to see me?"

"I asked what are you doing here. Answer the question."

"I'm here to pick up my daughter."

"Huh, I don't think so. Grace isn't ready to talk to you yet."

"Thank you for the information, Joe, but it's not for you to decide. Her little runaway number has lasted long enough. It's Christmas, and I want her home. With me. We're gonna celebrate like a family. You're welcome to join us. After all, our home is your home too."

"It's my father's home. I don't need an official invitation. I can show up whenever it pleases me."

She stretched her neck, trying to look past me into the cabin. "Where's Grace? I've missed her so much."

"When she is ready to see you, she'll let you know. Until then, go back home. I'm sure my father is worried about your whereabouts."

"Joe. Move. Grace is *my* daughter, and I'm not leaving here without her."

"How did you find us? There's no way you could've known where we were hiding."

"You two think you're smart and everything, but you forgot to cover your tracks."

"Our phones?"

"No. Car GPS. Philip installed one on every car last year. All I had to do was crack his password—which, by the way, should be changed because anyone could guess it, really—and voilà. I had access to your itinerary and exact location. I hope your father protects his assets better than his computer." She let out a high-pitched laugh that froze the blood in my veins. "Now, move. I'm her mother; she owes me obedience. Always."

Grace came to stand on my right, her posture guarded and her stance rigid. "Mom, I'm not coming home. Not yet. I don't wanna see you."

"You're not still sulking over the wedding day, are you? Over that piece of junk you called a gown? The one you ruined in yet another attempt to rebel against me?"

"Wow, I knew you were heartless, but this is a new low, Clarissa." I angled myself to face Grace, blocking Clarissa's view of her daughter. "You should go upstairs and work on your designs. I'll deal with your mom."

Her brown eyes widened, and I noticed the tears building in them. "You sure? I can give her a piece of my mind. I'm not afraid of her. I've been doing this all my life."

"Yes. Go. I feel like giving her a piece of *my* mind. She's upsetting you. Don't let her bad mojo affect your creative process. Not tonight. I'll come to get you when the coast is clear."

Grace cast a glance at her mother and nodded. "Fine. Kick her out. You have my permission." I kissed the top of her head, and my fingertips lingered on her arm, tracing her skin until she pulled away, breaking the contact.

Not wanting Grace to overhear the conversation if her

mother and I got into a verbal fight, I stepped outside, shutting the door behind me.

"What's going on in there?" Clarissa's voice gritted on my last nerve. How could my dad share his life with her? "Once we return home, you two will be grounded. Take my word for it."

I crossed my arms over my chest, unable to reel in the sneer bubbling in my throat. "You actually know I'm twenty-three and you can't ground me, right? That I'm too old to deal with a stepmom and I don't owe you anything?"

Clarissa stamped her foot. "It's the principle of the thing. You knew the rules and you still disobeyed us. You ran away, skipped the wedding ceremony, the pictures, and disappeared for weeks. And you stole my daughter. I'm not liking the tone you're using with me. You're lucky your father convinced me not to call the cops on you two. I was this close," she brought her thumb and forefinger together, "to lodging a missing person report. Or to report a kidnapping. Philip knew where you were hiding the entire time. I'm just frustrated that it took me forever to figure it out on my own."

"My father knew, and he did nothing about it?"

"He said you two required some fresh air. An adventure. Some bonding time. And that you could use the break because you've been working too much. Can I see Grace now?"

"No. I'll tell her to call you in the morning if she feels like it. It will be her choice. Her decision." *Because she decides her decisions.*

"Joe, I've always respected you, but who are you? My daughter's protector? I don't think so. Don't make me call the sheriff. You're not allowed to hold a minor hostage against her will."

"Well, technically, I'm her brother. And you've

witnessed it yourself. Grace is here of her own volition. No one is harmed or in danger. No one kidnapped anyone."

She raised her arms in exasperation. "Do you possess a rehearsed answer for everything? Gosh, you're exhausting. Kids nowadays." She sighed. "To use your own words, I'm your *mother*, and I demand respect and to be let in. Now."

"My mother died years ago. You're nothing to me. Just the woman my father chose to marry. For your information, the booking is under *my* name. And I'm an adult, so you can't force me into anything. *Step*mother or not."

Clarissa would vaporize me if her eyes were weapons. "You know what, Joe? I'll find another way in. Keep guarding the door like you're some sort of superhero."

She turned around and circled the house, probably looking for another door. Sadly for her, there was only one access, and I was blocking it.

Desperate to go back inside, I turned the doorknob. Nothing.

Shit, it was locked. How did this happen? Using my shoulder and all my weight, I pushed into the panel, but it didn't budge.

I knocked, praying Grace could hear me from the bedroom upstairs.

I heard a loud noise inside, something sounding like a crash, just as Clarissa's cries pierced my eardrums. "Joe, what is this? Is the house on fire?"

"Fire?" I walked in her direction when I noticed the flames licking every surface from the living room window. "*Nooo*. GRACE."

Returning to the front door, I kicked the panel, but nothing.

I patted my pockets for my phone but realized I'd left it inside.

"No. *No, no, no.*" I tugged at the roots of my hair.

"GRACE." Could she hear me? Why wasn't she coming to the door? Was she knocked out? Had she choked on the smoke?

I moved back and looked up to search the second-floor windows, but she was nowhere to be seen.

My heart hit the walls of my chest cavity. This couldn't be. Where was she?

"Clarissa, call for help."

She didn't react, hypnotized by the blaze, not moving.

"Fuck."

My pulse spiked.

"GRACE." The lining of my throat hurt.

Even if a neighbor called the fire in, the firefighters would never get here in time to save her. I had to think fast. Flames exited the roof now. The gingerbread house would burn down, taking with it the only girl I'd ever loved.

I coughed. My eyes stung from the smoke thickening the air.

I had no time to think. I had to act. And fast.

Behind me, Clarissa came out of her stupor and screamed at the top of her lungs.

"Clarissa, call 911."

No reaction.

I couldn't count on her. She was of no use, frozen by fear.

With my arms stretched above my head, I grabbed the lowest branch of the big tree near the burning house and lifted myself up. All my life, I'd been a musician, not an athlete. Even though I hit the gym every week, I wasn't the most skillful climber out there. I would do just about anything to save this girl, though.

I reached the second branch, avoiding looking down as the tree shook beneath my weight. Two more feet up, and I'd be able to steady myself enough to try kicking the bedroom window until it shattered. I had no idea if the plan would work, but I was willing to try anything. Even if it meant breaking my neck in the process.

"Clarissa, call for help," I hollered from my perch. "Please."

She stood still, now in a fit of tears.

Pushing on the tips of my toes, I gripped the branch above my head and swung until I could lock my legs around its girth and sit on it. *Almost there.* I had done it. Now, all I had left to do was to break in through the bedroom window that was at least four feet away. My blood ran cold. How was I supposed to pull that off?

A head peeked through the smoke. "Grace."

I motioned her to open the window so I could jump inside and save her.

She nodded and disappeared. *Where was she? Ohmygod. Where did she go?*

Seconds felt like eternity.

How did Grace, in a short period of time, become an extension of me, a piece of my heart? I couldn't tell. But this couldn't be the end. Our story hadn't even begun yet.

A chair crashed through the window. For a fraction of time, relief flooded me, but the oxygen fed the flames, and their intensity increased. Even from a distance, the heat burned my skin. My eyeballs itched from the dryness.

"Grace?"

Where did she go now?

Not thinking it through, I pushed back and then sprang forward, using the tree branch as a pendulum to climb through the window.

Smoke choked me.

My eyes teared, and I could barely see two feet ahead.

A small hand caught my arm, and I relaxed, despite the danger surrounding us.

"Fuck, I thought I had lost you."

I pulled her into my arms. "We"—my throat itched, and I tried to swallow to ease the pain lodged there— "gotta get you out of here."

"Not without you."

"I'll be right behind you." I kissed the top of her head.

She handed me DH, and I shoved the kitten into the pocket of my hoodie.

Lifting Grace into my arms, I helped her reach for the tree branch. "You gotta hold on tight, okay? Don't let go unless your feet are planted on the branch below. Don't"— another fit of cough—"do anything stupid. I'll push you to give you some momentum. It will help you reach the trunk."

She nodded. Once Grace's hand wrapped around the branch, I pushed her hips. Her ankles locked around the lower branch, and seconds later, she descended to safety. I blew out the air left in my lungs.

From the ground below, she beckoned me to join her.

Using the same chair she'd shattered the glass with, I climbed onto the windowsill, suddenly very aware of how much I hated heights. I reached for the branch but missed. My balance gave out, and I fell backward, my head hitting the floor with a loud thud. Dizziness swam through me, and when I stood up, pain bloomed at the base of my skull.

I heard Grace screaming my name, and it shot me with a new dose of adrenaline.

Climbing back onto the windowsill, I knew I had only one chance left to save myself. I braced to jump, ignoring the consequences, when a man appeared on a ladder below, helping me reach the first step. Where had he come from? How much time had passed since I first noticed the fire? I blinked, struggling to see past the thick smoke that choked the air, my eyes stinging as I climbed down the rest of the ladder.

"GRACE?" I called out her name. Where was she?

Paramedics and firefighters neared me. Lost in the moment, I hadn't noticed their arrival.

Did I pass out when I hit my head minutes ago? And if I did, how long had I been out?

Only then did I notice the small group of onlookers at the edge of the driveway, watching the cabin go down in flames.

"GRACE?"

Why wasn't she answering?

I used the back of my hands to rub the curtain of smoke that seemed to have attached to my eyeballs, blinding me.

My heartbeat deafened me.

My head pounded where I had hit it.

My body felt weak, yet I couldn't stop. I had to find her.

"GRACE?"

A man came to me. "Son, you need to let us examine you."

"No. Grace. Where is she?"

"The young lady?"

I bobbed my head. "Yes." My voice strained. My eyes burned. Exhaustion invaded me. "I wanna know where she is. I need her. I-I love her."

"She's getting oxygen. Follow me. We'll get you on it too."

"No need." I yanked away from the fingers gripping my upper arm. "I'm fine."

"Son. Your hands. You gotta let us bandage them. And put an oxygen mask on you."

"My hands?"

"Yes."

"What about them?" Still in a daze, I looked down.

It felt as if someone had ripped the ground from under my feet.

My hands were covered in burns.

"How? I don't feel anything." I turned my palms around as the reality of it hit me like a freight train. "I-I'm a pianist. That's my…That's my job. My…huh…life." Heart-wrenching sobs poured out of me. "I can't… It's not…"

"It's the adrenaline. Once it wears off, it'll hurt like a bitch. We'll give you something for the pain. It may look worse than it is."

Tears I didn't know I possessed streamed down my face.

Music was my life. The only thing I really excelled in. I had no idea how not to be a musician…a pianist.

Numb, I followed the paramedics to the ambulance. I felt so tired right now.

"Grace?" I mumbled as he helped me lie down on a stretcher. "I need her."

"As soon as she's done, I'll find her for you."

Chapter 15

"Joe." Grace's tears had left streaks on her soot-covered cheeks as she sliced through the crowd. Her hair was a mess, strands flying in all directions. Her white sweater was smeared with dark stains.

Grace stood a foot away from me, cupping her heart with one hand as more tears rolled down her face when she saw my bandaged ribs. Turned out I had cut my left side when I jumped into the blaze through the broken glass and would require stitches. "Ohmygod, you're hurt."

The paramedic, who had been taking care of me, lifted the oxygen mask from my face. I forced a smile, trying to ignore the state my hands and body were in for now.

"Come here, you." My voice sounded as if I had smoked ten packs of cigarettes a day for years.

Grace shook her head. "I can't. I'm scared I'm gonna

hurt you more." She scanned the length of me. "Your ribs. Are they broken?"

"Nasty cuts. I'll be fine. You won't hurt me, just come closer. I need you right now. I thought I had lost you. I really did believe…" Emotions drowned my words. I turned my head toward the paramedic. "What time is it?"

"It's Christmas day."

"Grace, I need you to stand right by my face."

She stepped closer and did as I said.

"Okay, lean forward because I gotta tell you a secret."

She brought her ear close to my mouth. "Happy birthday." She cocked her neck, surprise flashing in her gaze. Before she could utter a word, I captured her lips with mine. My tongue pushed into her mouth, caressing hers in slow strokes. I wished I could tangle my fingers into her hair and hold her close, but with the bandages covering my hands, they were useless right now. She kissed me back like I was her only source of oxygen. We didn't need those masks to breathe when we had each other.

"Joe, I don't… We can't… You said…"

"Forget anything I said before. Don't ever miss out on doing something you want because it scares you."

"I'm not scared."

"Then kiss me back because I'm done fighting how I feel about you. I-I love you, Grace. I think I've been in love with you since I saw you dancing on that stupid bar counter."

"Wasn't I the first one to tell you I love you that night?" she teased.

"Maybe, but I'm the one making it official."

She cradled my face with her small hands, her eyes boring into mine. "What about our parents? Our stepsibling relationship? Isn't it frowned upon to date your stepbrother?"

"I don't care about what people say. Never did. Not going to start now. Anyway, for me, you've never been a sister. You've always been the girl I was falling for but couldn't have. Since your age doesn't matter anymore, I'm not wasting any second not telling you how I feel."

"And how do you feel, Joe?"

"I'm in love with you. I can't picture my life without you in it. Permanently. The last few weeks we spent together, they solidified the feeling. *My* feelings. Grace, I'll be yours for as long as you'll have me. I thought I would lose you tonight. Life is too short not to go after what you desire."

A fresh batch of tears welled up in her eyes. "Good, because I'm already yours. Always have been. My heart is yours. And you're mine, Joe Crawford. All of you."

She brushed her lips against mine, taking her sweet time.

My entire body vibrated, and I deepened the kiss. This, us, was the only thing that made sense tonight.

Clarissa's voice acted like a cold shower, bursting our love bubble and shattering the words we'd just exchanged. "Stop. Both of you. This is disgusting. Joe, remove your filthy mouth from my daughter's. And I don't know what drug you two used, but you can't date your sibling. It's illegal. And wrong. For the love of God, please stop kissing. It's troubling. You both need professional help. Philip, say something."

Grace and I broke apart. "Dad?" I searched the crowd around us for a familiar face amid the commotion

My father came out of his wife's shadow and neared me.

"When did you get here?" I asked, noticing the wrinkle etched into his forehead. Dad had his concerned face on.

The same one he sported back when my mother had been diagnosed with cancer.

"Just about now. Clarissa called me, but I was already in town. How are you doing, son?"

I swallowed the rock stuck in my throat. "I'll survive."

"Joe, your hands." My dad inspected the bandages. "How bad?"

I was glad he couldn't see the extent of the damage underneath them right now.

"Your hands?" Grace echoed. "Oh no. How have I not noticed them?" She kissed me on the lips. "I'm so sorry. I can't believe you hurt your hands. Are they burned?"

My heart swelled with emotions I wished I did not feel. "Yep." I cleared my throat. "Both palms and most fingers."

Her eyes brimmed with tears, and it fractured my heart as worry painted her face.

"Baby, don't cry. It's gonna be okay. Don't worry about me."

She nodded, and I prayed I could believe my own words too.

Inside, though, I was coiled tight as fear lodged in my heart.

Now that some of the adrenaline had left me, I hurt everywhere. And I was afraid my hands would never be the same again. That they would never work their magic again.

The medication they injected me with couldn't numb the full intensity of the pain radiating through my fingers and arms. If I could still feel my hands, perhaps the burns weren't that extensive, and there would be no nerve damage. A guy could only hope.

I focused all my attention on my father. "Not sure which degree. It's better you can't see it. It doesn't look good. I'll try to not panic until I see the doctors."

"I'm so sorry," Grace cried against my side.

"We'll get you the best care. I swear." Dad watched the firefighters at work. "Anyone can tell me what happened here?" he asked.

Grace stood upright and wiped away her tears. "Mom arrived unannounced, and I refused to talk to her. Joe took it upon himself to deal with her. I heard them going at it outside, and I wanted to put a stop to their fight. When I reached the last step, the Christmas tree fell by the fireplace and caught fire. DH…huh, our kitten…got scared and started running around all over the furniture. He tripped over the bottle of wine on the table. The alcohol dripped onto the floor, and soon the table caught fire too. Before I could react, the entire place was burning down. I tried to pull the tree away from the fireplace, but it was too late. Flames surrounded me. I had no way of escaping, so I went back upstairs. Then I remembered DH would be afraid, so I called him until he figured out it was safer for him to come with me than stay downstairs and risk getting burned alive. When I went back up, I couldn't see a thing. Smoke blinded me. It took me forever to reach the bedroom window, and that's when I saw Joe on that tree. Coming to my rescue."

"Enough." We all turned to face Clarissa. "Everyone is safe, the house is gone, *blah blah blah*. What I wanna know is why you two were eating each other's faces just now?"

No one said a word. Grace moved closer to me, combing my hair back with her fingers as I lay on that stretcher.

"Philip? Aren't you gonna say something? After all, it's your son we're talking about."

My father eyed his wife, then shrugged. "All I'm seeing right now is two young people who have fallen madly in love with each other. I don't see why it should matter.

Grace is smart enough to make her own choices. And knowing my son, I'm pretty confident to say he never touched her before she turned eighteen." My father locked eyes with me. "Please tell me I'm right."

"We didn't kiss until just now. Sure, the attraction has been there from the start, but we didn't act on it." He had to know I spoke the truth. If we excluded the night we first met. But that didn't count. She was Isla then. Besides, we both paid the price for it. Living in a constant state of lust and not being able to do anything about it was punishment enough.

"Philip, you have to put a stop to it. Your son could be arrested if someone presses charges. He's not allowed to date a minor. Not in the state of Tennessee. And not under my roof either."

My father checked his watch. "Clarissa, it's Christmas Day. Grace is officially eighteen. Nothing we can do about it now." He winked in our direction. "Come on, give them a break. We'll meet them at the hospital."

"I can't believe you're defending their actions. They are kids. They have no idea what they're doing."

He pulled her further away.

"Tell me, how did you find me?"

"Same way you found the kids. The GPS on the car."

"Think they're going to stay married?" Grace asked once they were out of ear reach.

I shrugged. "At this point, I don't really care. Our future is ours. I won't meddle in their business if they don't meddle in ours." Something moved against my stomach, and I remembered DH in my pocket. "Hey, Grace? If you could get your hand down my front, I think you'd like it."

She slapped my shoulder. "Oh god, you're such a pervert. This isn't the time, Joe. No matter how tempting it is now that we're officially together."

"I wish. But it's something else." I winked, and she cast her eyes down with a smile. She looked adorable with her smoke-streaked face. "A package. Come on, palm it. It's desperate for your love. And to be pet."

"Seriously, how can you think about sex when you're hurt?"

"With you, I'm pretty sure sex will be on my mind all the fucking time. Right now, though, I'm not talking about my dick. I swear. Someone else needs your affection, baby."

Once she did as I asked, she found our kitten hiding in my pocket. "You got him out? Ohmygod, I thought we had lost him... Forever."

"He's our first baby. I would never leave him behind. How bad a dad would I be if I did?"

"Don't say things like that. I don't wanna picture you as a dad. Not for another ten years."

"Ten years? Are you serious?"

"Six?"

"I don't care. As long as you picture a future with me too."

Chapter 16
Grace

"What did the doctor say?" Philip asked as I joined him and my mother in the waiting room. "Want me to talk to him?"

I tried not to fall apart in front of them, but inside, I was barely holding it together now that I wasn't by Joe's side. They had sedated him, and he was sleeping. "A…a mixture of second- and third-degree burns all over both hands. They don't know the extent yet." A hard lump formed in my throat and I blinked back tears. This was bad. "He-he's got stitches across his ribs due to the lacerations when he jumped through the…the window." Philip opened his arms, and I sobbed as he held me. "I-I'm sorry. It's all my fault. He tried to… He tried to save me."

"Honey," Philip said. "Joe will never regret saving your life. Whatever it may cost him. I swear he would agree with me if he were awake. Don't blame yourself. None of this is your fault."

"I knew you two running away was a bad idea." My mother shook her head beside us. "I should have come to get you sooner."

I stepped back, facing her. "When it comes to me, nothing with you is ever a good idea, Mom. You disagree with everything I am and everything I do. You've been tearing me down for eighteen years. I can't do this anymore. You and I, we're done."

"Grace Marguerite Sullivan, I won't let you disrespect me. I'm done with your bratty behavior."

"Bratty? Can you hear yourself right now? I'm wondering who's being difficult here. I did nothing wrong. I just needed to breathe away from you. Because being your daughter is not an easy feat. I can't live with the pressure anymore."

"And you think falling in love with your stepbrother is a sign of maturity?"

Was she serious now? "It has nothing to do with maturity. I love him. Enough to give my life for his. And from what I've witnessed tonight, he would give his for me too." I clenched and unclenched my fists at my sides. "I'm sorry, Philip," I said, returning my attention to him. "I wish you two a Merry Christmas, but I'm not going back home with you. I just can't. All my life, I've been struggling to be accepted by my own mother. For the first time in my eighteen years of existence, I'm unapologetically happy. I love Joe, and he loves me. We're both adults, and nothing you two say will change anything. I'm done living with unrealistic expectations that don't belong to me. I'm my own person, and I intend to shine on my own terms from now on."

"Grace." My mother spoke through gritted teeth. She barely ever used that tone with me. "You're gonna do what we tell you to."

"No. I'll find a way to finish high school and be independent. I'm done being miserable. All thanks to you."

I turned on my heels, blocking her voice out. The one asking me to respect her and to listen to her orders.

"I was hoping you'd be here when I woke up," Joe said when his eyes landed on me. "I've missed you."

"How could you? You were asleep."

He smiled at me. "Still. Sleep is boring when you're not around."

"How do you feel?"

"Like my hands caught fire." He winked. At least he hadn't lost his sense of humor.

"It's not funny. You can't say that."

"It hurts. But now that you're here, it feels all better."

I leaned in and kissed him. "Thanks for saving my life."

"Anytime. I would do it all over again." He perused the room. "Seen my dad?"

"Yep. In the waiting room. At least he was, a few hours ago. I got into a fight with my mother and left them there."

"Grace… I've been thinking about it for a while, and I wanted to ask you… Promise me you won't freak out."

"Huh…okay."

"If you agree, maybe you could come to live in New York with me?"

"New York? With you?"

"Let me finish. You could finish high school there. And they have some of the best fashion design programs in the country you can apply to. You're so talented. I've seen you at work. You are focused, dedicated, and your creativity knows no boundaries. When you are accepted to NYFI, they'll be lucky to have you."

"I haven't even applied yet."

"You will, and you'll get in. All you gotta do is want it more than anything."

"But… All my hard work has gone up in flames. Pun intended."

"So what? You'll start over. It's gonna be even better the second time around. I'll help you. Cheer you on. Model for you. Whatever you need, I'll be there every step of the way. And then, at night, I'll make sweet love to you to show you just how much I love you and how proud I am of you."

"But what if…you know…your hands…" I couldn't find it in me to say it out loud.

"We'll figure it out. Together. I'm a fighter. No matter what, I'll push through it. We're gonna be fine."

"Our parents won't let us. My mom is already going batshit at the idea we're together."

Joe half-sat, propping himself up on his elbows, and kissed me. "She'll say yes. Let me deal with it. Only if you think it's a good idea… Otherwise, no stress. We'll think of something else. I don't like the idea of your living under the same roof as her when I'm not around. She's toxic."

I kissed him back. We both smelled like smoke and burned wood. "I love you."

"I love you more." He lay back. "Get my father, please. It's time I have this discussion with him."

"Are you sure?" Panic swirled in my stomach at the thought he and his father would argue about me.

"It will be all right. Trust me, I have your back."

I nodded. "I do trust you."

He grinned. "I know. Find him for me."

"Okay."

For the next twenty minutes, I paced the hallways of the hospital's Burn Unit, about to dig a groove into the linoleum floor with the soles of my sneakers. No way would I go back to the waiting room where I knew my mother would be.

When Philip exited the room, wrinkles surrounded his eyes. He looked tired. And somehow older.

"Grace, you can go back in. I have to talk to your mother first, then I'll come find you afterward."

I twisted my hands before me. "Am I in trouble?"

"No. I learned things about Clarissa's treatment of you I need to tackle with her. In private." He pressed my shoulder with one hand in a comforting gesture. "I don't want you hurting. Never. I'm sorry I didn't realize what was going on under my roof sooner." He sighed. "And for what it's worth, while we're at it, I'm glad Joe has you. You brought my son back, Grace. He's happier than he's been in years. I have you to thank for his change of attitude." Emotions filled his eyes. With a hand, he messed up his hair and looked away for a second. The simple gesture reminded me so much of his son right now. Philip looked like he was carrying the weight of the world on his shoulders right now. "We met with the doctor, and I have faith his hands will heal. We-we'll talk later, okay? Then we'll all go to bed. I booked a hotel down the road. Got you your own room."

"Thank you."

"It's the least I can do, honey."

He disappeared after he passed through the double door, and I returned to my boyfriend.

"Have you talked to my dad?" Joe asked as soon as I sat next to him.

I swallowed. "Yeah. He said he'd take care of it. Whatever you told him, thank you for having my back."

"Anytime, baby."

"Any news when you can get out of here?"

"They're keeping me for the night. The doctor wants me on IV for a bit longer. I should leave in a day or two, but I'll require medical care to change the bandages and stuff." He motioned me to come closer with his chin. "And I might require you to keep me busy while I heal. Think you're up for the challenge?"

I snickered. "Are you planning to take advantage of me, Mr. Crawford?"

"Yup. Fully."

I sat next to him, resting my head on Joe's shoulder. "When they release you, I'd like for us—"

A wheezing sound coming from the pile of Joe's clothes set on a chair in one corner of the room made me realize I had forgotten DH was sleeping there. I was surprised he hadn't woken up yet.

I scooped up the bundle of fur and settled back, holding it close to Joe, who nuzzled his head. "Baby, I can't believe he's been here all this time."

"Where did you want me to put him? We're homeless for the night. Your dad got me a hotel room. I wish you could share the bed with me. I don't like being alone. And after tonight, I'm not sure I'll enjoy the darkness ever again."

"I know. Just for a night, okay? Then we'll make up for the lost time. Dad is driving your mom to the hotel. He'll come back to pick you up once they're done talking."

I sat beside him on the bed. "It's not the Christmas I had in mind."

"It's not the birthday I had planned for you either. We'll have a do-over, I promise."

I snuggled by his side. "Don't worry. We're alive. That's all that matters."

"Not good enough for me. I wanna celebrate you. Turning eighteen is a big deal."

A loud yawn exited my mouth.

"You should sleep until my dad gets here." He scooted to the side to make room for me. "Come on, make yourself at home."

"You sure? Last thing you need is my hurting you more."

"Grace, you don't have it in you… To hurt people."

I lay by Joe's side and pulled the covers over both of us. "You wake me up if you're in pain or I'm taking too much space, okay? Or if I press against your wounds. Or—"

Joe kissed me silent. "Stop. Close your eyes. Don't over-think it. I'm fine. We're fine."

"Yeah."

"Now let's sleep. You must be exhausted."

I woke up sometime later to the sound of Philip and Joe whispering. For a second, I wondered where I lay. "Come on, Grace. Let me drive you to the hotel," Philip said, helping me up. "You deserve a good night's sleep and a real bed."

I rubbed my heavy lids with my fists. "What time is it?"

"Almost five in the morning. I'm sorry it took so long."

I focused my attention on my boyfriend. "How are you feeling?"

"Like I wanna rub my hands against concrete because they're itchy."

"Did you sleep at all?"

"Like a baby. You were here. That made it all better." He shifted on the bed. "Now go. I'll call you when… huh…never mind, we both lost our phones in the fire. I'll have the doctor reach out to you when I'm being released."

"You sure?"

"Yes. Love you." He kissed me, and I melted inside. It felt weird with Philip standing next to us, but I wouldn't trade my happiness for anyone, so I pushed the thought away.

"Did you find a litter box for DH?" I asked my stepdad.

"Yes. Everything is ready and waiting for you in your room. Come on, Joe needs his rest too."

On the drive to the hotel, I asked Philip the question that had been nagging me. "Did you talk to my mom?"

I wasn't sure I wanted to open that can of worms, but I had to appease my mind.

"I won't lie to you, Grace. We talked. She admitted she's been hard on you. I won't defend her actions because I don't agree with them. But I love your mother, and underneath the confident and ruthless personality she projects, there is a little girl who's been hurt too a long time ago. I'm not asking you to forgive her now or ever, but sometimes seeing both sides of a situation helps to understand stuff we couldn't before. I told her you needed time. And she agreed to give it to you. She's not happy about it but will respect your wishes. If you need help—professional help—of any kind, please let me know so we can figure it out together. Your mom agreed to seek help too. I just hope one day you two will be able to mend the past."

"Thanks. For…for all of it. Nobody ever took my side before. Only you and Joe."

"We're family, and family helps each other." He parked the car, and we both climbed out. "Wanna know a secret? When my first wife died—Joe's mom—I put all my energy into my work and neglected him for a while. He started acting out. For a long time, I blamed myself for my son hurting. Eventually, we sought outside help, and things got better between us. All this to say it's never too late to turn things around. Give it some time."

"Can I ask you something else?"

"Always."

"Do you really think Joe will be able to play the piano like he used to?"

He said nothing for a long moment. "The truth?"

I nodded.

"I do. It may take a while, but when that kid sets his mind on something, he won't let go until he's done everything in his power to make it happen. As long as the nerves aren't affected, I don't see why he wouldn't be able to play the piano again."

"Thanks. For your honesty."

"Good night, Grace. And happy birthday. We'll celebrate it later. I'm glad we had this chat."

"Me too. Night."

Chapter 17
Grace

I admired the space around me. White walls, high ceilings, and small windows. It was the same apartment he'd shared with his best friend while attending college, and with other roommates afterward, once Anderson moved out. Most furniture was secondhand, but it gave this place its character. My boyfriend had transformed the second bedroom into a workshop for me so I could prepare my portfolio for my college application. He even put DH's bed in a corner, a sign shaped like a fishbone that said "DH's room" hanging on the wall beside it.

Standing in the kitchen to grab snacks, I wanted to pinch myself. I was living in an apartment in freaking New York. Part-time, but still.

What meant a lot more to me was that I shared it with my boyfriend. Even to my ears, it sounded far-fetched. The same guy I met in a dive bar a few months ago. I had

Philip to thank for enrolling me into Cordera Academy on such short notice. Not my first choice, but it was part of the deal. I didn't get to have a say about the high school I would attend, and in exchange, I could enroll in the program of my choosing next year in college. Moving here came with another bunch of conditions I had agreed to. Nothing too bad or restrictive. At this point, I would've said yes to almost anything, as long as it meant not living under the same roof as my mother.

She and I hadn't talked since the night of the accident, almost two months ago. I wasn't ready to forgive her this time. Eventually, maybe… But she would have to do the work first and face whatever events from her past had turned her into the heartless woman I grew up with.

Joe hadn't returned to Broadway yet, still recovering from the fire's damage to his hands. He attended rehabilitation sessions every week to improve dexterity and rebuild strength in his hands.

Scars would remain on his skin, but the doctors were hopeful he would regain full mobility in both his hands.

Since I lived in the dorms at Cordera Academy on the weekdays, I spent all my weekends here with Joe and our fur baby whenever I wasn't working at the bookstore on campus. This was one more step toward the independence I had been craving for so long.

And I had never been so happy before in my life.

"Babe, are you coming back, or do I need to come get you?" Joe teased from the living room.

"Coming. Want anything else while I'm at it?"

"Nah. You. You're all I need."

I returned to his side, and he pressed play on the remote. We'd been playing video games for two hours. I had no talent, but he liked teaching me, so I rolled with it.

He said it helped him with his fingers' mobility, and his doctor agreed. Joe spent most of his free time at home these days, and I knew my presence between these walls made things less sour. I was on a winning streak when he paused the game and stared at me.

"What?"

"I love you."

I felt my cheeks warming up. "I love you too."

"No. I'm serious. You've been dealing with my sorry ass for two months."

I pressed my palm to his face. "Your sorry ass makes me happy. I have to pinch myself every day to make sure I'm not dreaming."

He pinched my side.

"Ouch. Why did you do that?"

"So you know it's all true."

I slapped his arm away, but seconds later, he lifted me until I straddled him.

"Oh no." I shook my head, not believing what I just realized.

"What?" His brows bunched together.

"Dick's Hole. You named our baby Dick's Hole? Are you kidding me?"

Joe burst out laughing. "Gosh, it took you forever to guess it. I thought it was fitting. It's where everything began. You, me, our story. Now that bar's name will always mean something to us. It won't just be the crappy place where we met."

I locked my arms around his neck. "When you say it like that, it almost sounds romantic."

"It is. Because it's us." Joe laid me on my back on the couch, his body hovering over mine. His lips teased mine in slow kisses that had my toes curling and my pulse spiking.

The air around us was charged with awareness.

I was panting, and all we'd been doing so far was kissing. "Can you show me just how much you love me? I need to feel you all over me. Tomorrow I'll be at the academy, and Friday will take forever to roll in."

"If it were up to me, you'd live here full time. Not in a stupid dorm."

I peppered kisses all over his face. "That's the only reason I was allowed to move here in the first place. It's a matter of a few more months. If I'm accepted to NYFI, we'll be together all the time. You might even get tired of me."

"Never." I felt him growing harder, his erection pressing on my lower belly, and I ground against him, searching for the delicious friction only he could provide my body with.

"Fuck me. Here and now. On this couch." I batted my eyelashes. "Please."

A loud growl left his mouth, and it vibrated through me. "I thought you'd never ask."

"Who's the liar now? You know each time you put your filthy paws over me, all my defenses melt away."

His mouth claimed mine, stealing every molecule of oxygen meant for my lungs and shutting me up as his tongue danced with mine, igniting each nerve cell in my body. "I'm so in love with you, Grace Sullivan."

Within seconds, our clothes were scattered across the room, and I was breathing fast, combusting just at the way my boyfriend eye-fucked me.

When he kneeled before me and his tongue laved the seam between my thighs, I swore I saw stars. My fingertips dug into his skull as one of his digits found its way to my heated center. "I knew pianists were skillful with their fingers," I said, recalling what I had told him that night in the bar. "But this..." He worked his magic, and a loud whimper parted my lips. "More." My voice sounded like a plea.

He accelerated the pace of his fingers, and soon I was floating, the ecstasy shooting through me about to rip me apart in the best kind of way.

"Ready to be fucked like a woman now?" The desire shining in his eyes rendered me speechless. "So? I won't do it until you say the word."

"Fuck me until I can't remember my own name. Until I can't walk straight and I'm yours forever." I winked, knowing the effect the words would have on him. Joe Crawford was the sweetest and most caring boyfriend in the world, but when he got you naked, he tipped your world upside down without blinking.

He possessed you with each thrust of his hips.

He infiltrated himself into each crevice of your heart with every kiss.

"Show me what you've got," I teased.

And that was exactly what he did. For hours to come.

We ended up skipping dinner and going straight to dessert. Until we were so spent that neither of us could answer the door when the food delivery guy rang the buzzer sometime later.

"Grace, I think we should buy handcuffs."

"Hmm, that sounds sexy."

He kissed me. "Not what you think. Their only purpose would be to keep you here with me. If you're handcuffed to our bed, you will have nowhere to go, and I'll be able to get a taste whenever I'm hungry. What do you think?"

"If you can wait until I graduate, then I'll be a willing participant. As long as two can play this game."

"Awesome. I'll be able to add *boy toy* to my resume?"

I chuckled. "You need more hours of practice for that title to be recognized. I'll decide when it's a done deal."

"Challenge accepted. We'll see who calls it quits first."

"Bring it on, *boy toy*."

He tickled my ribcage "You're gonna beg me to stop, Grace."

"Never. My determination knows no limits."

Epilogue
Grace

"To you, baby," Joe said, pouring champagne into two glasses and offering me one. "You did it. You officially graduated with a degree in fashion design. I'm so proud of you. I'm still amazed by your talent and the fact your version of the jacket-gown has won you the *Designer of the Year* award. It was long overdue." He leaned in and kissed me, his tongue pushing into my mouth and stealing my breath away.

From the night we met until today, my boyfriend had always found ways to sweep me off my feet. Over the years, he'd always been my idol. His dedication, his commitment, his sense of humor, and his love that knew no boundaries. I adored every single thing about Joe Crawford. Whatever he did, I was his biggest supporter and would forever be.

"My mother would die if she knew it was the project I presented for the final fashion show."

Our relationship had improved over the years. After Philip persuaded her that letting me move to New York with Joe after the accident was a good idea, she had cut all ties with me. I had learned later she went to therapy during that time. For eating disorders and other mental health issues. Mom had been raped when she was a teenager by a famous fashion photographer, and it had impacted the rest of her life and her self-image. I hadn't forgiven her for all the pressures she had put on me throughout my short existence, but we could at least spend time together nowadays without wanting to kill each other. She was only allowed to compliment me. I didn't know whether it was her husband's idea or her therapist's, though, but I played along because it was good for my own self-image too. No matter what, I had Philip to thank for all of it. If he hadn't stuck by her side and been there to reassure me when I needed him to, no doubt our relationship would have burned to ashes at the same time the gingerbread house did. Over the years, he had become the parental figure I always dreamed of. And the one I needed.

We still weren't a happily-ever-after family, but there was hope for all of us.

"I love you," I said against my boyfriend's mouth.

His lips curled up. "That's perfect because I have a surprise for you. A graduation present. It's for us, but I thought I'd make it official once you had your diploma in hand."

"What is it?"

He stared at me, seriousness taking over his face. "First, I think we should go back to Mistletoe Creek."

As if the mention of the little town summoned him and he knew I'd need his comfort, DH butted my leg and licked my fingers when I picked him up.

"Why? Are you sure? Last time we were there... Let's

just say it's filled with memories I'd rather never revisit." I took Joe's hand between mine, tracing the scars the burn had left on his skin with the tip of my finger. The scars that would forever remind us of that night. "You could have died that day or lost the ability to play the piano. And I could have been burned alive. Not sure going back is such a good idea."

He stepped closer to me and enveloped me in his arms. "Too bad because I think it's a wonderful idea." I said nothing, waiting for him to continue. "It was the place where I came to the realization that no matter how much I tried to resist you, I was fucked because I loved you too much to let my fear drive you away. Where I decided the risk of loving you was worth much more than the one of never taking a chance on us. It's time we make new memories there. You said to me once you wish you could live there full-time." He fished a set of keys out of his pocket and placed them in my palm.

"What are those for?"

"The keys to our future. We'd still have to travel back and forth for now, but one day soon, it will be our forever home."

"You bought a house there?" I blinked, not sure I heard him right.

"No, I bought us a home. The cabin we stayed at."

"What about the fire damage? They were extensive. The last time I talked to Lea, she said they never fixed the place. It had been sitting empty for years."

Joe kissed my forehead. "It turns out I know a guy who knows a guy…"

I slapped his chest. "Oh gosh, now you're talking like a real small-town guy."

"Anyway, now that Andy is friends with Carter Hills,

the country music superstar, I have connections in the area. And long story short, his brother-in-law, or someone like that, owns a construction business in Green Mountain. I met with him a few times—nice guy, by the way—and he agreed to renovate it for us. He added a back door, a porch, and a balcony on the second floor, accessible through the master bedroom. It's brand new. And it's ours."

"Are you serious?"

He nodded. "Yes. Nashville is Music City and an upcoming fashion destination. We could both work there if we decide to. It's not even a three-hour drive. We'd live close to Andy and Abby, and we could keep the cabin as a weekend retreat and get an apartment in town. Lots of possibilities. Atlanta is close by too. And New York and LA are just a short flight away." He tucked my hair behind my ears, studying my reaction. "What do you think?"

My heart pounded in my chest.

Deep down, I was still in love with Mistletoe Creek, and I had kept contact with some of the people we met there that winter.

"Wow. It's…wow. I'm speechless."

"Is that a yes?" Joe watched me, waiting for my approval. "We can keep it as a vacation home too. I just thought it would be fun to go back there. It will always play an important part in our love story."

I bobbed my head multiple times. "I want it. I want everything with you. Now and forever. I love you, Joe Crawford." I jumped into his arms, my legs locking around his back as I kissed him senseless. "You're the best man I've ever met and my best friend. Who would have thought we'd go back to Mistletoe Creek one day and own a piece of property there?"

He shook his head, kissing me back. "Nah. I think you meant the real question is, who would have thought the girl I met in a bar that night would turn out to be my forever girl?"

Time stopped as we lost ourselves in each other, not giving a thought about the world still spinning around us.

Bonus Epilogue

Joe

I watched Grace from the corner of my eye, our fingers intertwined, as I kept a death grip on the steering wheel with my other hand. Her gaze flicked to mine, and I could read the anxiety swimming in her irises. Bringing our joined hands to my lips, I kissed her knuckles. "Babe, it's gonna be fine. Don't worry."

She watched me with big eyes, nibbling on her bottom lip. "I'm trying not to worry. I swear this"—she gestured to her face with her free hand—"is my way of trying to be chilled about the entire thing."

I offered her a warm smile and hoped it erased some of the discomfort she felt. "Do you trust me?"

She sighed and dropped her shoulders, relieving some of the tension straining her back. "Yes. You know I do. Joe, you're the only person I fully trust with everything. Since the night we met, I've never *not trusted* you. Even when I wanted to hate you when you started acting like a prick afterward."

"Then breathe and enjoy the night, okay?"

"Yeah. I'll try. I just hope everything runs smoothly."

"We left to grab a bite forty minutes ago. Everything was perfect back then, and everything will still be when we return."

"Are you sure we really thought of everything? What if we forgot something?"

"Grace. It's all gonna be fine."

She inhaled, looking like she was psyching herself up. The same way she always did before any important event in her professional life.

After her creations grazed the front covers of countless fashion magazines, Grace had made a name for herself in the business. It'd been three years since she graduated from New York Fashion Institute.

"Is your dad already there?" she asked after a moment.

"Yes. They arrived twenty minutes ago. He texted me while you were on the phone earlier."

"Maybe we shouldn't have gone to dinner. I should have stayed there…"

"Babe, you've spent over forty hours there in the last three days. So, eating wasn't an option but a necessity. You've been running on snacks and caffeine for far too many days. It's unhealthy. Food is fuel, and fuel is important if you don't want to faint in the middle of your special night."

"Fine. I guess you're right."

I flashed her a bright grin. "I am. I always am, no?"

She scrunched up her nose. "Don't inflate your ego."

I quirked a brow.

"Fine, you're often right. When it concerns me. Happy, now?"

"Yep."

"Good." She remained silent for a full minute. "And you know what? You might be right again. I can do this. I really can do this."

"Yes, you can. That's the spirit. For what it's worth, I'm proud of you."

She leaned in, and I kissed her lips before bringing my attention back to the road.

"I love you," Grace said, relaxing against me, her cheek pressed against my shoulder. "Thanks for dealing with my nervous, wrecked self."

"Anytime."

I parked in the reserved spot by the back door and killed the engine.

"Ready?" I asked, rounding the car and opening the passenger door, offering Grace a hand.

"As much as I'll ever be."

Grace

We entered the shop by the back door, and I felt a flush creeping up my cheeks at the sight of all these people who came to see me tonight. Well, not me, but my work. My creations. The ones I'd worked so hard to put out into the world.

Last spring, when Joe and I bought a house in Tennessee and decided to split our time between Mistletoe Creek and Nashville, I ended up meeting Dahlia Ellis. She had been a household name in country music for years after founding the Carter Hills Band with her best friend back when they were just kids. She was an international rising star when she decided to retire from the music industry. Her life took a turn for the worse, and she'd had a few bad years before she decided to reinvent herself and open a bridal boutique in Green Mountain, the town next to Mistletoe Creek.

Her husband Nick was the one who rebuilt the gingerbread house after the fire that turned it to ashes back when Joe and I vacationed there together for the first time.

Since then, we'd met a few times and bonded over fashion. Last year, Anderson, Joe's best friend, took part in a charity concert and for the first time in almost a decade, Dahlia walked onstage with her ex-bandmates for a surprise performance. We all ended up at the same after-party, and she offered me a chance to design an exclusive gown line for her boutique.

It took me a total of two seconds to accept, right before I started freaking out because this felt like a dream.

Fast forward to a year later, and here I was, about to unveil my collection at Dahlia's Bridal Shop in Nashville.

Even though we met hundreds of times and exchanged more emails and phone calls than I could recount, the idea of being here with Dahlia Ellis still felt like a surreal experience.

Addison, Dahlia's best friend and event planner for tonight, came up to me. "You look beautiful, Grace. Are you ready for the big reveal?"

Joe, probably sensing my nerves, squeezed my hand.

"Yes." I exhaled. "I think I am."

"Good. The media representatives, the influencers, the bloggers, and the photographer we hired for tonight, are all here. The bar has been set in the front corner, and servers are already passing *amuse-bouches* around. I saw the collection when I arrived, and it's better than everything I had imagined. No doubt it's going to be a success. You can be proud of yourself." She switched her attention to Joe. "The piano is yours when you are ready." She turned to leave but stopped mid-stride. "I met with Eleanor. She looks as spectacular as her mom. I'll leave you to it. Come and see me in five minutes so we can do this."

Addison left us alone, and I tried to relax.

"You should get ready," I told Joe.

"Only if you're okay." He studied my face. He always made sure I was fine. And I liked that about him. Joe was a bit territorial when it came to me, and after everything we went through, I loved the idea he always had my back when I needed him to and gave me space when I required some time to myself.

I sighed. "I am. I will crush it."

He kissed me and left me alone just as Dahlia walked up to me and squeezed my hand. "You're going to do amazing, Grace."

Emotions built in my eyes. "Thanks for everything you've done for me in the last year. It's more than I ever thought possible. Growing up, I had no one in my corner. Until I met Joe, I was all alone. And now"—I gestured to the space around us—"this is my life. And I have you to be thankful for."

She rubbed my upper arms in a comforting, maternal gesture. "It's all you. You have the drive and the talent. I'm just helping you to showcase it to the world."

"Still, it's much more than I ever hoped for. Thank you."

"You're welcome. I can see us doing great things together in the future."

I swallowed the lump in my throat. I still couldn't believe Dahlia Ellis was giving me a chance.

"Go shine, Grace. It's your night."

Dahlia signaled Addison, and soon the party planner walked to the microphone set at the front of the store, a large smile brightening her face. "Thank you all for coming tonight," she said. I blocked the sound of her voice, focusing on Joe as he sat by the piano, and we exchanged more with our eyes than any words could.

He nodded at me, and the little crowd applauded at something Addison said.

Next to me, Dahlia grabbed my hand in hers and led me forward. "Come on, it's your cue."

Addison introduced me, and after I said a few words, which I was sure I would never remember because I was a nervous ticking bomb, I moved aside as two models we hired for the night walked the makeshift runway, presenting some of the pieces I designed.

Joe played the piano, his focus on me, and I could sense the heat of his gaze on my back, which appeased every cell in my body.

Later, people were mingling, drinking, and enjoying finger food, and I watched them with a sense of pride I never felt before.

I had given three interviews, answered too many questions, and posed for numerous pictures.

"Honey, I am so proud of you," Philip said, leaning in to kiss my cheek. "This is spectacular. You did great."

"Where's Ella?" I asked. I hadn't seen Eleanor since I was first introduced.

"Your mother went to clean her up after her clothes got soiled."

As if summoned, my mother approached and kissed my cheek. Our relationship had improved over the last two years. It still wasn't perfect, but she was now making an effort. "It was beautiful, Grace. That emerald-green gown is a gem. It's going to be a hit. I have no doubt." The fact my mother could now recognize my worth and the value of my work meant a lot to me. Never could I have imagined us getting to that point in my life—she complimenting me instead of trying to rip me apart.

"Thanks, Mom."

Two little arms stretched in my direction, a drooly smile, aimed just for me. "*Mamamama.*"

I picked Eleanor up and kissed her chubby cheek.

My little girl had turned five months old two days ago.

She was my pride and joy. And the Christmas present Joe and I never saw coming.

She had her daddy wrapped around her tiny fingers, and she was the best part of both of us.

Speaking of her daddy, Joe closed in on us, pulling me against his side. "How are my girls doing?" he asked, kissing both our cheeks.

Eleanor giggled at the sound of his voice.

"We're ready to go home," I said. "Tonight was magical, but I'm exhausted."

"My girls' wishes are my commands."

We said our goodbyes to everyone, and when I passed Dahlia, I hugged her for a long minute.

"I'm so proud of you," she said. "Tonight was a success. I can see a lot more of those nights in your future. Get some rest, and enjoy your weekend. We'll talk on Monday."

"I will."

Anderson and Abigail neared us next, followed by Riley Burns and Carter Hills, Dahlia's former manager and her best friend slash ex-bandmate. We exchanged a few words before leaving the shop.

A satisfied smile played on my lips, and I had no idea how to erase it. In all honesty, I never wanted it to fade away.

Eleanor had fallen asleep in Joe's arms, and I watched them, feeling at the top of the world.

"We should get married," I blurted out.

Joe halted and turned to face me. "You serious?"

I nodded. "I think it's the next step. It feels right."

He blinked and stared at me. "I thought you wanted to wait a little more."

With a shrug and a shake of my head, I met his gaze. "I'm done waiting. I'm happy. I'm in love. I have a family. And a job I'm passionate about. The only thing missing is calling you mine."

"But I'm already yours. Always have been." He leaned forward to kiss my lips. "We're it, baby."

"I know. But I want to call you my husband."

"Let's elope."

I laughed, not sure whether he was serious or not. When he pulled back and our eyes locked, his expression told me he wasn't kidding. "You sure? Our parents will never forgive us."

"Who cares, right? It's us. Running away isn't new. We'll celebrate with the ones we love and care about afterward. I want Ella and you there with me. You're the ones who matters the most to me. I don't care about anyone else."

I blinked. "You really are serious?"

"Yes. We have the weekend off. Let's go to Las Vegas and make it official."

"You really want to do this?" I asked, just to make sure I heard him right.

"Grace, I've been calling you my wife for years. It's about time you agree to it too."

Tears welled up in my eyes. "I love you, Joe Crawford."

"Well, I love you more, Grace Sullivan soon-to-be Crawford. Let's go and get married."

Eleanor's eyes fluttered open and she watched us.

"You want mommy and daddy to get married?" my future husband asked.

She blinked once, then clapped, her smile so contagious it pulled one from me too. As if she agreed to our happily-ever-after too.

Thank you for reading Grace and Joe's emotional and beautiful love story.

Whose story will you read next?

Snowbound - Anderson Ford's story
emmanuellesnowshop.com/products/snowbound

False Promises - Carter Hills's story
emmanuellesnowshop.com/products/false-promises

Sweet Agony - Dahlia Ellis's story
emmanuellesnowshop.com/products/sweet-agony

Last Hope - Riley Burns's story
emmanuellesnowshop.com/products/last-hope

ACKNOWLEDGMENTS

When I was invited to write a Christmas love story, how could I refuse, right?

From the moment I first penned SnowBound in 2021 (it was a novella back then), I knew Joe had to have his own story someday. I just didn't think it would be a Christmas one.

But then, as I finished the last rounds of editing of SnowBound, Joe took more and more space in my head, and I knew he had to be the hero of my next book. Then Grace appeared on the pages, and I fell in love with her. Big time. Her heart, her vulnerability, her strength.

And *Wicked Love* was born.

Joe and Grace stole my heart from their first encounter, and I'm so happy you get to read their story now.

We all feel insecure from time to time, and having someone in our corner who pushes us to be better and believes in us is priceless. That is Joe for Grace, and Mr. Snow for me. I hope you have that special someone in your life too.

Do you wish Mistletoe Creek was a real town? I know I do. There's just something magical about that place. And it's next door to Green Mountain, so what's not to like? And seriously, a gingerbread house cabin is kinda cool, no?

Thank you, Breanna Lynn, for inviting me to be part of this project. I'm grateful.

Thank you to Gail Haris, Ember Davis, Sasha Marshall, Mae Harden, Alina Lane, Claire Hastings, January Rayne, Aria Wyatt, and Willow Sanders, the other Mistletoe Creek authors. You ladies, rock. I'm proud to be on this rid with all y'all.

Thank you to my kids and husband for being there and giving me space when I'm dealing with a tight schedule and deadlines. We're about to go on an adventure, and sometimes it feels like we don't have enough room for all of us, but somehow, we always make it work. I'm amazed by us, guys. And I can tell the next year will be filled with little and big joys I'll remember for a long time.

Thank you to my editor, Shalini, for fitting Wicked Love in between all our other works in progress. When you told me I should do a Hansel and Gretel retelling, I wondered for a moment how to bring it to life in a romantic kinda way, and I'm so happy with how it turned out.

To my Snowmate team, thank you for being by my side with each release. Anni, I'm so glad we finally met in person. You were my first bookish friend when I moved to town, and I'll cherish our afternoon together forever.

To the Bookstagrammers, YouTubers, TikTokers, bloggers, and everyone else who love my books and help spread the word, thank you from the bottom of my heart. You guys are amazing, and I'm happy you're on this adventure along with me.

To my readers. I love you all. Thank you for everything. Every single one of you is truly special, and I love reading each of your emails and messages. They always put a smile on my face. Thanks for your love and support. Always.

Wicked Love is a wrap. Always believe in yourself. And don't let other people's insecurities prevent you from reaching for your dreams.

With much love and gratitude,

Emmanuelle

WANT MORE EMOTIONAL LOVE STORIES?

WHICH COUPLE WILL YOU PICK NEXT?

False Promises

★★★★★ "The angst, the utter heartbreak, and protectiveness I felt for Carter during this book is unreal!"

★★★★★ "Emmanuelle Snow really knows how to tug at all of your emotions and does such a great job of bringing her characters to life!"

A gripping story of sizzling passion, lust, and the price of fame.
Start Carter Hills's story now

Sweet Agony

★★★★★ "If I could give more than 5 stars, I would."

★★★★★ "This is not a romance, it is a story about first love, first heartbreak and growing up."

A compelling tale of love, friendship, and self-discovery that will tug at your heartstrings.

Start Dahlia's story now

Cruel Destiny

★★★★★ "Wow. Just wow. If that could be my review, that is all I would write."

★★★★★ "Emmanuelle has done it yet again. She found a way to slip into my mind and heart with her words and the creation of characters you can't help but fall in love with."

★★★★★ "This book broke my heart in the first twenty five percent and sewed it back together."

A story of healing, second chances, and the risks of opening your heart to someone new. Can they trust each other with their hearts, or will their pasts keep them apart?

Read Nick and Dahlia's love story now

Wild Encounter

★★★★★ "This is by far one of the most well-written book I've read this month. It is dynamic, intriguing, interesting, unafraid to go there and most of all touching."

★★★★★ "I personally wouldn't call this book JUST a romance novel because it's so much more. I 100% recommend it no doubt in mind."

A tale of passion and perseverance that will leave your heart racing and your spirit soaring.

Read Tucker and Addison's love story now

Last Hope

★★★★★ "This book was not only about the darkness but it was about pure love, hope, spice, family, and friendships on point with just the right amount without overpowering the storyline at all."

★★★★★ "Devon and Riley's story is a beautiful one with a lot of emotions. The subject matter is intense but it is handled very gently."

A tale of resilience and second chances in a world where love and danger intertwine.

Read Riley and Devon's love story now

Midnight Sparks

★★★★★ "The characters, the love, the humor, the steaminess, the emotions… it's everything I hoped and more."

★★★★★ "I think that is one Emmanuelle Snow's sexiest novels yet."

Welcome to the island where Holiday magic meets unexpected romance and a chance at a fresh start.

Read Gavin and Aisha's love story now

Fallen Legend

★★★★★ ""The love that grows, not only through tough angst but through unconditional moments had my heart. This is a spicy and riveting book"

★★★★★ "Emmanuelle Snow doesn't just tell a story, she creates an entire world."

A poignant and uplifting journey of hope, love, and the power of second chances.

Read Sam and Madison's love story now

Snowbound

★★★★★ "5 big stars from me for this amazing story. Absolutely loved it!"

★★★★★ "Emmanuelle Snow's stories are always full of angst, and Snowbound is no exception."

The intertwined lives of two strangers bound by fate in the midst of a snowstorm.

Read Anderson and Abigail's love story now

All available at emmanuellesnow.com

ABOUT THE AUTHOR

Soulfully Beautiful Love Stories

USA Today Bestselling Author Emmanuelle Snow is an author of contemporary YA and women's fiction love stories, who gives life to strong characters who'll fight with all they have to reach their life goals and find their own happiness. She loves her characters to be relatable and realistic.

Emmanuelle is in love with love. Especially complicated, deep, and passionate feelings that make a relationship extraordinary and complex all at the same time.

In her spare time, when she's not writing or reading, she likes to go on road trips—with her four kids and her own soulmate—watch movies, paint, or do some DIY, always with a cup of green tea in her hand and listening to country music.

She splits her time between beautiful Canada and the small US towns she adores.

Find all of Emmanuelle's books here:

emmanuellesnow.com

Want to connect with Emmanuelle online?
YOU CAN FIND HER HERE:

Website
Author's bookstore and merch store

Snow's VIP newsletter
emmanuellesnow.com

Readers' VIP group Snow's Soulmates
facebook.com/groups/snowvip

amazon.com/author/emmanuellesnow

goodreads.com/emmanuellesnow

bookbub.com/authors/emmanuelle-snow

facebook.com/esnowauthor

instagram.com/snowemmanuelle

x.com/snowemmanuelle

pinterest.com/snowemmanuelle

tiktok.com/@snowemmanuelle

ALSO BY THE AUTHOR

CARTER HILLS BAND UNIVERSE

(suggested reading order)

Carter Hills Band series

False Promises

HEART SONG DUET

Blindsided

Forevermore

Whiskey Melody series

Sweet Agony

SECOND TEAR DUET

Cruel Destiny

Beautiful Salvation

BREATHLESS DUET

Wild Encounter

Brittle Scars

Upon A Star Series

Last Hope

Midnight Sparks

Love Song For Two Series

Lonesome Heart Duet

Fallen Legend

Rising Star

Two of Us Duet

Snowbound

Wicked Love

MEDORA BEACH UNIVERSE

Wrecked series

Cast Away

Ride For a Fall

Touchdown series

Kickoff

Read them all

emmanuellesnow.com

All available on author's bookshop

LAST HOPE

RILEY

Our eyes met. Something passed between us. Attraction. Recognition. Yearning. Maybe a mix of all three. And much more. I brought the tumbler to my lips, relishing the burning sensation of the whiskey as it slid down my throat.

A gear shifted inside me.

My heart did one of its moves. The one where it got all bothered and excited.

I fastened my grip around the glass in my hand.

The woman pushed her long, curled blonde hair over one shoulder, giving me a perfect view of her lickable, slim neck. *Lickable?* Was that even a word? I pushed the thought away. I was a man on a mission.

The vampiric side of me—the one I hadn't known existed until now—emerged in full force.

I blinked.

The temptation to bite the soft flesh of her neck multiplied by the second.

The woman smiled, and all my restraints broke loose. They caught fire and burned to ashes in the dark night.

I gave her a subtle nod as I continued staring, hoping for a slight hint of encouragement from her.

Her red-painted lips pursed as she mouthed *Hey* in my direction.

Smoothing my palm over my trousers, I made a beeline for her, my steps light and focused, not allowing the sea of people to break our eye contact. The air around us heated up. We were outdoors, but it felt as if someone had cranked up the thermostat. Slowly, I raked my fingers through my brown hair, gelled to perfection tonight, doing my best not to mess it up. From an outsider's point of view, I bet I looked in control—the opposite of how I really felt. No one in the business needed to know how unruly my heart was behaving. Or the tremble that had started in my fingers. The flickers of excitement that burned in my core.

A server passed by, and I discarded my tumbler before grabbing two champagne flutes from his tray.

In two long strides, I reached the woman in the red lace dress. Her smile reached her eyes when I offered her the sparkling alcohol. "To a great night and even greater company," I said as we clinked our glasses. "I'm Riley." I held out my hand for her to shake. Our palms met, and a jolt of heat surged through me, setting my insides ablaze in a way no woman ever had. Her touch alone threatened to make me combust.

"I'm Devon."

I lifted our joined hands to my lips and kissed the back of hers.

Her soft chuckle resonated through me. "I can already tell you're a gentleman."

"My mama taught me well. So, what brings you here, Devon? I've never seen you at one of these country music parties before."

"Oh, you go to these a lot? This is my first time. It's

quite intimidating. A friend of mine invited me, but she's running late."

I followed her gaze across the rooftop bar. Country music singers, songwriters, and musicians counted for more than half of the patrons here, and together, they'd won enough awards to fill an entire room. Woven through them were music producers, managers, movie stars, and their dates. Yeah, to someone unfamiliar, the crowd could easily appear impressive.

My man, Carter Hills, waved at me when my eyes drifted to him. I raised my glass in his direction. He was not only one of the biggest artists here tonight, but also one of my protégés and closest friends. Over the years, we rose to the top of this industry together, our friendship growing stronger with each album. We had each other's backs. Always.

"All these people, they aren't as intimidating as they look once you get to know them. Most of them are pretty great actually. Down to earth, and genuinely nice. Don't let their success make you nervous. Looking great is part of their job description. But there's much more to them. Well, to some of them at least."

The woman snickered and clutched my elbow, balancing her weight on her four-inch nude stilettos. "You seem like the kind of man who knows a lot about the country music scene, am I right?"

I took another sip of my drink and shrugged, my eyes trained on her face, enjoying the tilt of her red lips. "You could say that. I've been around these folks my entire life, but an active part of their world for almost a decade."

Devon's gray-blue eyes flared. "You're a country singer? Ohmygod, I'm sorry if I didn't recognize you." A flush crept along her neck and cheeks. The same neck I was still dying to feast on.

"Nah. I'm not. Believe me, you don't want to hear me sing. It may burst your eardrums. No kidding."

She grinned at me, and my heart swelled in my chest. "Who are you then? What's your superpower?"

"I'm a manager." I pointed to Carter, now deep in a conversation with Rita L. Sterling, a music producer. "I manage this fellow's career, amongst others."

Devon moved closer and lowered her voice to a whisper as if she feared someone would hear her. Not a chance with the chatter and music surrounding us. "Is that Carter Hills? I'm sorry. I'm not a groupie, I swear, but I thought I recognized him earlier when I walked in."

"Yeah, that's him. I can introduce you later."

She shook her head, the blush on her cheeks darkening. "No, you don't have to. I-I'm nobody here. I'm not part of this world. This night is surreal, I—"

A waitress bumped into my side and lost her footing, sending an entire tray of red wine glasses crashing all over me.

Time seemed to slow. I blinked as my clothes absorbed every drop.

"Oh, shit. I'm…I'm so sorry. It's…oh gosh, it's my first night here. I'm so, so sorry. I-I messed up. Wh-what can I do?" she asked, her eyes glistening with tears as she righted the now-empty wine glasses on the splattered tray. "Ohmygod. I ruined your shirt, sir. This is…this is so unprofessional. I'll get fired over this. Wait here, I-I'll be right back. I will…I'll get my purse. Dry-cleaning is on me."

I wrapped my hand around her wrist before she could run away and leveled my eyes with hers. "Stop. Breathe. It's just a shirt. I own a dozen more just like it. You won't get fired because nobody will say anything to your boss. I might even have been the one who bumped into you. I should've stood on the side of the deck. See? I'm standing in the way."

The waitress raised her watery eyes, studying me as if there was a *but* about to come out of my lips. There wasn't.

"What's your name?"

"Daph..Daphne."

"Well, Daphne. Breathe in. Breathe out. It'll help to calm your nerves."

She filled her lungs with a deep inhale.

"Yeah, like this." Her shoulders dropped. "See? Much better. Listen, now you go back there," I pointed to the bar, "fill this tray up, smile, and get on with your night. Don't let this little incident affect you. You're doing a great job."

She blinked and swallowed hard, a quiver of a smile trembling over her lips. "How-how can you tell? You don't even know me, sir."

"It doesn't matter. I'd recognize a hard worker anywhere. I have a flair for finding good people. It's my superpower." I fished a business card out of the inner pocket of my now damp jacket. "If waitressing doesn't work out or you're ever looking out for a job, gimme a call. I might be able to put in a good word for you. Don't worry. The sun always comes out after the storm."

"Wow…huh…thank you. I… This… That's the nicest thing someone has ever said to me." She clutched my business card, pressed it against her chest as if I'd just promised her the world. With a shy smile, she turned and walked away, chin raised and back straight.

Warmth filled me. Daphne would be okay. She just needed a pep talk. And I happened to be good at those too. Perhaps I possessed more than just one superpower after all.

Devon leaned closer, and her eyes widened in stunned disbelief. Her perfume wrapped around me, tipping my senses into a dizzy haze. She smelled like spring and rain. Fresh and flowery. I burned the fragrance to my memory. Even my heart seemed to enjoy it as it expanded in my chest and drummed faster.

"Wow. That was… That was amazing. Most people would have screamed at the poor girl or threatened to get her fired. Instead, you boosted her self-confidence. That's very noble of you. You are a good man, Riley."

I looked down and pinched the fabric of my stained shirt to unglue it from my chest. "Thank you. It was just a clumsy mishap. Now, would you excuse me for a minute? I need to freshen up." I grimaced as she grinned at me, the gleam in her eyes captivating me.

Her smile grew wider, and she gave a gentle nod. "Go ahead. I can't wait to see how you manage to come back still dressed in these clothes. This should be interesting." She wrinkled her nose at my drenched state and said, "Yeah, very interesting."

I smiled. Like a fool. There was no way I could hold it back. Falling under this woman's charm felt like breathing. Easy. Natural. And imperative. "Wait and see. I may surprise you. I always find ways to turn impossible situations around."

Devon chuckled. "I'm sure you do. While you are in there cleaning up, I'll order us more drinks. Whiskey?"

"On the rocks," I said, holding back a grin. Did Devon notice what I was drinking earlier? If so, it made her even more attractive. I dreaded walking away from her, not ready to escape the magnetism that had settled between us. "I'll be quick."

We eye-fucked each other for a few seconds, my pulse spiking at the way her eyes brought her whole face to life.

Full lashes, high cheekbones, straight nose, heart-shaped lips. She was every shade of beautiful. With just one glance in my direction, this woman had captured my heart the moment I first saw her. It made no sense, but I wasn't about to overthink it.

So far, our encounter was the highlight of my night—of my day, maybe even my week.

With a sigh, I broke eye contact.

In a hurry to get back to her, I weaved through the bar crowd, my jacket now open, my soaked shirt sticking to my abs, and the front of my trousers molded to my thighs. Nothing about being wet and dressed up felt good. I was pretty sure even my socks were damp. I frowned at my predicament, wondering how I was supposed to get through the night in clothes soaked with red wine. It wasn't as if I had a change of clothes in my car or something. It wasn't as if I could just run home and change, even though I lived less than ten miles away. Tonight, I had no intention of letting Devon out of my sight, even for just a few minutes.

In the men's room, I peeled off my once-white shirt, gave it a disapproving look, and dropped it in the trash. A complete loss. I couldn't save it even if my life depended on it. After dabbing my trousers with paper towels, I turned the undershirt around and tucked it into my pants. I used more paper towels to soak up the excess wine from my jacket and put it back on. The look wasn't perfect, but in the dark bar, nobody would look too closely to notice.

I eyed myself in the mirror one last time, fixed my hair and the lapel of my jacket, and with determination in each step, made my way back into the night, looking for the woman in the red dress.

Read Riley and Devon's story,

Last Hope, now

emmanuellesnowshop.com/products/last-hope

"Once again Emmanuelle Snow has created such amazing work. I went through an emotional journey with this story, I had happy tears, sad tears and laughter. It was just so heartfelt and pure. I couldn't put the book down." **(Goodreads)**

"I always love it when an author is able to make me feel all kinds of emotions. And with 'Hope and Country', Emmanuelle definitely managed that. This read was romantic, fun, sad, heartbreaking and wonderful." **(Goodreads)**